Refining
Felicity

Also by Marion Chesney

RAINBIRD'S REVENGE
THE ADVENTURESS
RAKE'S PROGRESS
THE WICKED GODMOTHER
PLAIN JANE
THE MISER OF MAYFAIR
FREDERICA IN FASHION
DIANA THE HUNTRESS
DAPHNE
DEIRDRE AND DESIRE
THE TAMING OF ANNABELLE
MINERVA
REGENCY GOLD
DAISY
ANNABELLE
THE CONSTANT COMPANION
MY DEAR DUCHESS
HENRIETTA
THE MARQUIS TAKES A BRIDE
LADY MARGERY'S INTRIGUES

Refining Felicity

Marion Chesney

St. Martin's Press / New York

Library of Congress Cataloging-in-Publication Data

Chesney, Marion.
  Refining Felicity / Marion Chesney.
    p. cm. — (The School for manners ; 1st)
  ISBN 0-312-02288-3
  I. Title. II. Series: Chesney, Marion. School for manners ; 1st.
PR6053.H4535R44 1988
823'.914—dc19   88-16888
                                                        CIP

Design by Glen Edelstein

First Edition
10 9 8 7 6 5 4 3 2 1

For Thelma Osmani

Refining
Felicity

Chapter 1

The great blessing of old age, the one that never
fails, if all else fail, is a daughter.
          The Reverend Dr. Opimian

All daughters are not good.
          Mr. Falconer
—*Thomas Love Peacock,* Gryll Grange

I T IS A SAD fact that one's insides do not
keep pace with one's outsides. Pains in
the lower back, wrinkles round the eyes, soft puffiness
under the chin, elasticity gone from the step; all the out-
ward manifestations of growing old make up a pitifully
hardening shell over the ever-youthful and hopeful soul.

Such was the case of the Tribble sisters. Each Season
came round with all the hopes and torments and joys they
had experienced in their teens. They were twins and no
one knew quite how old they were, but they were ru-
moured to have reached their half century. They still
dreamt of beaux, and later, after drums and routs and balls
and ridottos, in the privacy of their drawing-room, dis-

1

cussed each killing glance and hopeful pressure of the hand.

Euphemia, or Effy, Tribble had at least gained the false reputation of having once been a beauty. In her youth, she had been cursed with sandy hair, pale eyelashes, and a dumpy figure. Now her hair was a cloud of silver, her figure trim, and her eyelashes discreetly darkened with lampblack. Her delicate skin was only faintly lined and she had adopted all the mannerisms of a great beauty.

Her twin, Amy, was a sharp contrast. She was tall and square-shouldered and mannish, with a leathery skin and masses of iron-grey hair. She was flat-chested and flat-bottomed and had great flat feet which flapped along like boards. Effy often sighed over the fact that she, Effy, had turned down proposals so as not to leave her dear Amy alone, and Amy, who thought little of herself, half believed this fiction, although it was Amy who had turned down two genuine proposals of marriage out of loyalty to Effy—who had clung to her and cried and had told her that the gentlemen were only playing with her affections.

The fact that anyone at all had ever proposed to one of them was a miracle, for neither had any dowry to speak of. Their mother had died when they were young, and their father was a gambler who went to meet his Maker on a cloud of cigar fumes above the gaming tables of St. James's during a singularly bad run of luck.

The house in the country was sold to pay the debts. The sisters would not have dreamt of parting with the house in Town, for Town meant the Season and the Season meant marriage.

Such money as they had at their father's death, they had put in the bank, drawing on it as they needed. Neither would hear of investing it, regarding the Stock Exchange as just another variety of gambling hell. And so the years passed and the money dwindled. One by one the servants were paid off, until there was only a daily scrubbing woman left.

But they were kept merry with shared dreams, and added to that, they had hopes of financial security. Their aunt, a Mrs. Cutworth, who lived in Streatham and who was vastly rich, had promised to leave them everything in her will. For years now the sisters had been travelling to Streatham to visit the horrible old lady, who always seemed to be at death's door but would never pass through.

One November day, when ice glittered in the parks, and a red sun low on the horizon stared at sooty London with a baleful eye, the Tribbles set out in a hired post-chaise, trying not to count the cost of all the post-chaises they had paid for over the years to take them to Streatham.

Amy was warmly wrapped in a fur cloak. It was bald in places, but she had painted the bald spots with brown paint and hoped they did not show. On her head she wore a striped cap and on top of that a huge black felt hat like the kind worn by highwaymen. Effy was wrapped in so many trailing scarves and shawls, it was hard to make out what she was wearing underneath.

Soon the sooty buildings gave way to small sooty cottages and hoardings advertising Warren's Blacking—as if anything were needed to add to the general blackness. Blue shadows lay across the icy road in front of them as the sun sank lower. But they were warm with dreams of what they would do with the money when Mrs. Cutworth died.

"Coals," said Amy, flapping her great feet up and down on the carriage floor in her excitement. "We would have fires—even in the bedchambers."

"And a lady's maid," said Effy. "Oh, and proper servants."

"And three meals a day," said Amy.

"And dowries." Effy considered a good dowry more important than food or warmth.

Effy was soft and timid on the outside and had a hard core of steel within, the hallmark of a truly feminine woman. Amy was crude and harsh and ungainly and swore on occasion quite dreadfully, but could be sentimental and impractical to a fault. She used to give money to beggars until Effy stopped her from carrying any, to curb such misplaced and feckless generosity.

When their carriage lurched through the gates and up the short drive leading to Mrs. Cutworth's mansion, they saw the physician's carriage outside.

"Do you think . . . ?" began Effy eagerly.

"No, I don't think," said Amy curtly. "She's always calling the physician."

They climbed down from the carriage and Amy knocked at the door, a brisk tattoo which sounded through the house.

The door was opened by a moon-faced butler with a lugubrious expression.

"Sad news, ladies," he said in a mournful voice. "Madam has passed on."

"Gone out?" said Amy.

The butler pointed up. "She has gone to the angels."

Amy's fine grey eyes sparkled as she looked beyond the butler and up the shadowy staircase as if seeing a vision of roast-beef dinners, warm rooms, and servants waiting at the top. Effy quickly put a handkerchief to her eyes to hide her excitement.

"We shall pay our last respects," said Amy. The twins walked slowly up the steps, although they were tempted to break into a run.

The doctor was just coming out of the bedchamber. "Buttered crab," he said. "I told her not to touch it, but

4

she would have it, and it's been the death of her."

As the Tribbles walked into the gloom of the bedchamber, Baxter, Mrs. Cutworth's lady's maid, was just twitching the bed curtains back into place.

She was a tall, gaunt, elderly woman, and when she saw the Tribbles, she began to cry, great ugly sobs racking her body.

"There, there," said Amy. "It was not as if it was unexpected."

"Nothing," sobbed Baxter. "How could she do it to me? Not a brass farthing has she left me, her that promised me riches in her will."

"Do not cry," said Effy briskly. "We will take care of you, Baxter."

"What with?" demanded the maid rudely. "She's left you nothing as well."

Amy felt sick. "You are overwrought, Baxter," she said sharply. "How can you know this?"

The maid scrubbed her eyes with a corner of her muslin apron. "Because I read her will, that's why."

Effy pulled back the bed curtains and looked down on the dead face of her aunt. Mrs. Cutworth had a smile on her face, as if savouring their dismay and mortification.

"Where is this will?"

"In her bureau," said Baxter. "I'll show you."

She went to a flat-fronted bureau in the corner of the room and let down the flap. She took a roll of parchment tied with pink tape from one of the pigeon-holes and mutely held it out.

Amy seized it and, followed by Effy, carried it to the window and jerked up the blind. Pale grey light crept into the room.

With Effy peering round her arm, Amy read in horrified silence. Mrs. Cutworth had left all her worldly goods to a Mr. Desmond Callaghan.

"Who is Mr. Callaghan?" she asked.

"A Fribble," said Baxter sourly. "A Pink of the Ton. Been calling for over a year."

"Why didn't you warn us?" demanded Effy sharply.

"I didn't take it seriously," said Baxter. "He used to flirt with her and she'd laugh at him behind his back and say he was only after her money."

Amy's hands tightened on the will. She noticed with irritation that her last pair of good gloves had a split on the index finger of the right hand. "I have a good mind to destroy this," she said.

"I thought o' that," said Baxter. "But she's sent a copy to her lawyer. You could challenge the will. Mr. Callaghan isn't a relative. You could prove he only called to gull her."

"It would take money to fight this in the courts," said Effy. "And her lawyer would say she was of sound mind."

Baxter began to cry again. Amy patted her awkwardly on the shoulder. "I'll give you a good reference, Baxter, and if the worst comes to the worst, you may come and starve along with us."

The sisters sat in silence as the post-chaise bumped over the frozen ruts on the road to London.

At last Amy said passionately, "Bad cess to her. I hope she died slow."

"Tch! Tch!" admonished Effy, shocked. "It may be God's judgement on us. We never liked her, you know. We only pretended to like her to get her money."

"That is not entirely true," said Amy harshly. "We were kind to her. We put up with her spite and humours. We were the only living relatives she had. As far as we knew, the money would have come to us whether we visited her or not. We *did* go out of duty, and you know it! She was cruel and insulting to us. And yet, you know, quite a big part of our motive in seeing her was because we were sorry for her. She seemed so bitter and lonely. Besides, what ways are there for two gently bred women to find money? Society allows us only two options: marry, or wait for someone to die. I wish I were dead myself. No one is going to marry either of us."

Effy began to cry. Amy had at last voiced the hitherto unmentionable.

Amy put an arm about her sister's shoulders. "I'm a beast. Of course someone will marry *you*. You're awfully pretty. The deuce! There must be something. What have we got to sell?"

"Nothing," wailed Effy. "There is nothing left."

"There's the house."

Effy looked stricken. She would rather die of starvation at a good address than live genteelly at an unfashionable one. She began to cry harder than ever.

"Oh, dear. Forget I spoke," said Amy desperately. Then her face lit up. "By George! We have got something to sell. We can sell ourselves."

"As courtesans?" asked Effy, drying her eyes and looking more cheerful at the prospect of a really interesting fantasy. "We could be like Harriet Wilson and have the Duke of Wellington paying for our services."

"No, no. We can be chaperones. Look here! We have the right connections. We are good ton."

"You can't eat good ton," said Effy crossly.

"Listen. There are many counter-jumpers and mushrooms who would pay for the chance of getting into society."

"But how do we find these people?" asked Effy. "I mean, it might take ages and ages. We don't know any common people."

7

"We advertise. Damme. We advertise. Just like Warren's Blacking."

A few weeks later, Mr. Benjamin Haddon stood hesitantly on the pavement outside the Tribbles' home in Holles Street. He felt lost and strange. He had been away from London for many years. He had worked long and hard for the East India Company, until a trifling service to a rich raja and the resultant munificent reward had given him fortune and freedom. Before turning into Holles Street, he had walked along Oxford Street, dazed by the glitter of the shops. He wondered if the crowds who swarmed down it ever thought of the time, not so very long ago, when it was a dismal trench of a road, a Via Dolorosa, along which the unfortunate were taken to the Triple Tree, as the scaffold at Tyburn was called. It was estimated five hundred thousand had gone to their deaths on that terrible scaffold, but now it looked as if it had never existed. Everything was new and different. Even fashions had changed. The ladies wore next to nothing, and he found it hard to tell prostitute from gentlewoman. That was why he had thought of the Tribble sisters. He was sure *they* would not have changed. They were a fixed part of his memories of the London he had known before he sailed to India.

Although he had been a not-very-well-off young man, he was of good family and had been invited to various social events. But his clothes had been sadly countrified and the ladies were apt to shun him. All except the Tribbles. Amy and Effy Tribble could always be counted on to look delighted when he asked one of them to dance. In his innocence and still wrapped in fond memories of his youth, Mr. Haddon did not realize the Tribbles would have been delighted to dance with anyone at all, both the girls being tired of the long evenings spent with the other wallflowers. He remembered them as being safe and friendly. He wondered if they were still alive and still lived in Holles Street. But the brass plate at the door, dating from the last century, before street numbers were invented, said TRIBBLE quite clearly. He knocked at the door.

At first he did not recognize Amy, who answered it. All he saw was a tall, raw-boned woman wearing an ugly cap and with a sacking apron tied over her gown.

They stared at each other in silence. Amy saw a very tall, thin, slightly stooped man in a plain but expensive coat. His pepper-and-salt hair was combed back and tied in the old-fashioned manner at the nape of his neck with a ribbon.

"Is your mistress at home?" he asked. He held out his card.

Amy read the inscription and then blushed. "It is I, Mr. Haddon. Miss Amy Tribble. No wonder you did not recognize me. It is the servants' day off. Come in, come in."

But I wouldn't have known *him,* thought Amy. I remember him as he looked all those long years ago. He was kind, as I recall, and of good family, but quite poor.

She ushered him into the drawing-room, where Effy was sitting before the empty fireplace, wrapped in so many shawls that only the tip of her cold-reddened nose peeped out.

"Effy, dear," said Amy. "This is Mr. Benjamin Haddon. You remember? He went to India."

Effy shed several shawls and held out a hand for Mr. Haddon to kiss. "Delighted," she murmured. "We last met at the Chumleys' ball, as I recall. I was wearing a white slip with a gold key pattern, very fine, and I had, let me see, three plumes on my head."

"You have grown more beautiful, Miss Effy," he said

gallantly, "while I have become stooped and quite yellow."

"How was India?" asked Amy, wondering whether to go downstairs and decant the last precious bottle of port.

He smiled. He still has his own teeth, thought Amy, as we have. How very odd. One does not often see people of our years with all their teeth, and yet here are three of us. "It was very hot," he said. "Colourful and violent. I dreamt so often of grey skies and soft rain, I am distressed to find I cannot get my bearings now I am back. That is why I came to see you. You were both kind to me when I was a penniless young man. But how do you go on? Is your father alive?"

"No, Papa has been dead this age."

Effy cast a few more shawls and began to fan herself, her blue eyes flirting over the top. Amy thought sourly it was just like Effy to bring out a fan when the room was as cold as a tomb.

Mr. Haddon glanced about him. He noticed that there was very little furniture and no ornaments or knick-knacks whatsoever. There were cleaner squares on the dingy wallpaper showing where pictures had once hung.

"I am become quite rich," he said abruptly. "You must let me help you."

Two pairs of shocked eyes stared at him. Both Tribbles were bound by the iron laws of convention. It was quite *comme il faut* to wait for an elderly relative to drop dead, or to marry someone one did not like in the slightest in order to get money—but accept charity? Never!

"I am afraid we have given you a false impression," said Amy. "We are shortly to become working women, so you have no need to pity us."

"What kind of work?"

Effy produced a folded and much-thumbed copy of *The Morning Post* and pointed silently to an advertisement. He took out his quizzing-glass and read it carefully.

"And have you had any replies?"

"Not really," said Amy, throwing Effy a warning look. They had had two replies, but the families who had called were patently put off by the cold rooms and lack of servants.

"Let me think," he said. "I believe you have put in the wrong type of advertisement."

"What do you mean?" cried Effy, forgetting to flirt.

"In this age of sensibility," he said slowly, "parents often ruin their daughters by indulging their every whim. You have seen some of the difficult ones. They are so spoilt, so hoydenish, that they do not 'take.' Now, if you were to advertise for difficult misses, parents who were absolutely desperate might reply . . . if you see what I mean." He coughed and added tactfully, "The middle classes are apt to equate riches with good ton. An aristocrat would not notice, provided he thought he was gaining the correct schooling for his daughter before the Season. After all, one of your favourite phrases used to be that you always made the best out of the worst."

There was a long silence. Effy looked at Amy, wide-eyed.

"By Jove!" said Amy suddenly. "I believe you have it." She rushed out of the room to return with pen and paper.

"I will take it myself direct to the newspaper," said Mr. Haddon. "At least let me do that for you."

The three of them worked busily, writing and scoring out and redrafting until they were satisfied.

"That should fetch them," said Mr. Haddon at last. They all looked at the finished result.

If you have a Wild, Unruly, or Undisciplined
Daughter, two Ladies of Genteel Birth offer to
Bring Out said daughter, and Refine what may

have seemed Unrefinable. Religious and Social Training. The Seeds of Decorum planted where the Ground was Once Considered Barren. We make the Best of the Worst.
Direct to XYZ, Cruickshank's Perfumier, 12, Haymarket."

The perfumiers ran a letter collecting service for advertisers.

"I shall take it away directly," said Mr. Haddon. "We shall meet tomorrow."

After he had gone, Amy said dismally, "We shall have to tell him the truth. We can't go on saying the servants have a day off."

"He is a fine-looking man," said Effy dreamily. "Did you notice the speaking look in his eye when he bent over my hand?"

But, for once, Amy would not share in any romantic speculation. "I had better go down to the larder and see if I can scrape up something to eat," she said. "We go to Lady Rochester's tomorrow. Be sure to eat as much as you can, Effy."

"Oh, I shall. But do not disgrace me again."

"Whatever do you mean?"

"You know what I mean, Amy. You scandalized the Petersons at their party by trying to stuff so much food into a reticule the size of a trunk and were caught. We were never asked back."

"It seemed like a good idea at the time," said Amy sulkily.

She spent an hour in the kitchen trying to coax scrag-end of mutton into a nourishing stew. A rumbling from the street outside made her leave the pot and go up the area steps. A coalman was bent over their coal-hole. Behind him stood his cart, laden with sacks of coal.

"Leave that alone," said Amy sharply. "We did not order any coal."

"Mr. Haddon ordered and paid for it," said the coalman crossly.

"Very well," said Amy. "I had forgot." She ducked back down the area steps.

There was a warm glow in her heart. Another man might have sent them flowers or chocolates. Only clever Mr. Haddon would think of sending them coal. If he had asked if they would like any coal, the sisters would have refused. That would have been accepting charity. But this! This was a present.

Amy went down to the empty cellar and stood with her hands clasped and her eyes shining, waiting for the avalanche of coal to descend down the chute from the street above.

Two days later, in the county of Sussex, the Countess of Baronsheath sat at a pretty escritoire in her drawing-room. She slid out a drawer and took out a copy of *The Morning Post*. She read the Tribbles' advertisement over and over again. Could it be a joke? Were these self-styled Ladies of Genteel Birth really genteel? Could anyone in the whole wide world reform her daughter, Lady Felicity Vane?

There were halloos and cheers from outside. She crammed the newspaper back in the drawer and went to the window. A party of young bloods on horseback, headed by the countess's daughter, Lady Felicity, were riding through the rose garden. A Scottish gardener like an infuriated gnome was jumping up and down and howling at their disappearing backs in a fury.

Lady Baronsheath sat down again, her legs trembling. What on earth was she to do? Felicity's first coming-out ball was that very night, and instead of beautifying herself, she was tearing up the rose garden with the noisiest of the male house guests.

It was all her husband's fault, thought Lady Baronsheath bitterly. He had wanted a son, he had always wanted a son, and she had not been able to give him anything other than one girl. So he had proceeded to treat the girl as if she were a boy, and he had indulged her every whim. Now he was all set to sail to America for an extended visit, leaving his wife to take Lady Felicity up to London for her first Season.

And there should be no need to do that at all, thought Lady Baronsheath crossly, with such a marital prize on the doorstep. The Marquess of Ravenswood, their neighbour, had recently returned from the wars. He was handsome, elegant, and rich. He was a trifle old, being in his thirties, and Felicity was nineteen, but surely an older man was what she needed to curb her. All Lady Baronsheath's dreams of seeing her daughter engaged to the marquess on the night of the ball had long since vanished. The marquess had already met Lady Felicity and appeared to despise her, and his very presence always seemed to make Felicity worse.

Sometimes the sheer exuberance of her husband and daughter made Lady Baronsheath feel faded and washed out. The house was an elegant one, quite modern, built in the Palladian style, with graceful wings springing out from either side of the classical main building. The rooms were light and beautifully furnished. But the whole place always smelled of damp clothes and horses and dogs. Felicity rode almost every day, always dressed in men's clothes.

The ball was to be held in the chain of state saloons that made up the first floor of the central building. Already from above came the faint strains of the orchestra, re-

hearsing a waltz. Lady Baronsheath tried to console herself with the thought that a Felicity in evening dress and
with her hair up would perhaps appear enchanting in the
marquess's eyes and that, with luck, he had not heard of
her reputation for being the hoyden of the hunting field.

She did not think so, but she had to hang on to that
hope to give her courage for the evening ahead.

Chapter 2

And now the dreaded country first appears;
With sighs unfeign'd, the dying noise she hears
Of distant coaches fainter by degrees,
Then starts and trembles at the sight of trees.
—*Soames Jenkins,* The Modern Fine Lady

LADY FELICITY VANE MEANT to behave well. She had noticed her mother's anxious face, her worried looks, her nervousness over the success or failure of this ball. So Lady Felicity had made up her mind to look as beautiful as possible and to flirt and simper like the very best of daughters. She would charm this Marquess of Ravenswood and accept his hand in marriage. All young ladies tried to marry well; all good misses owed that much to their fond parents. Besides, if Lady Felicity married Ravenswood, then she would not be taken away from her beloved hunt. Priding herself on her practical mind and never pausing to think that the marquess might have other ideas, Lady Felicity, with unusual and alarming docility, allowed her maid, Wanstead, to prepare her for the ball.

Wanstead had withstood Lady Felicity's humours longer than most. She was a tough elderly countrywoman with few graces and a hide like leather. In the past, nurses had come and gone, and then a succession of governesses, driven away by Lady Felicity's practical jokes and wild behaviour, but Wanstead had remained for three years now. Her greatest asset was that she was hard of hearing. The noise of Felicity's tantrums did not disturb her, and she had developed a bobbing, weaving motion from learning to avoid thrown hairbrushes, curling tongs, and other missiles.

Felicity adored her father and tried very hard to behave like the young rip he would have liked for a son. She had once put on a very pretty gown with frills and lace to please her mother and her father had laughed and laughed and had said she looked like an organ-grinder's monkey. This was the first time since that humiliating time that Felicity was making any effort to look like a young lady.

Patiently she sat before the toilet table while her hair was pomaded and curled, while she was scented and powdered.

She was a tall girl with thick black hair, a thin, tanned face, and large greenish-grey eyes. She had a generous mouth and a deep bosom. She was not beautiful by fashionable standards, which demanded a plump, dainty figure, a dimpled face, and a tiny mouth. She had high cheekbones, a great disadvantage in an age where women wore wax pads inside their cheeks to achieve a Dutch-doll look. But with her black hair dressed in a Roman style and with her thin and athletic figure attired in floating white muslin, she managed to attain a certain regal air. Good health gave her skin a glow and made her hair shine with blue lights.

Felicity had her instructions. She was to wait until the guests were assembled in the hall and then descend the staircase. The staircase was a double one and she was to walk down on the right-hand curve, one hand resting lightly on the banister, and with her head held high. A footman would follow her, holding a branch of candles. Felicity was now quite excited at the idea of making an entrance. And at the back of her mind, although she did not quite know yet what it was, was the hope that her father, seeing his daughter as an attractive young lady, would give up his longing for a son. Although he doted on Felicity, he always made her feel as if she had usurped the place of that dream-child.

She had caught a glimpse of the Marquess of Ravenswood the day before, when she had been out riding. Some of his men had been digging a drainage ditch on Plump's field on his property. As Felicity rode past, the marquess, who had been giving instructions, took off his coat and seized a spade and started digging himself. She noticed, not for the first time, that he was tall and powerfully built. A lord who was not too high in the instep to dig his own ditches would make an amiable husband. Felicity thought of a husband as being someone like her father, who would allow her free rein. She knew that romance did not enter into an aristocratic marriage. Their lands bordered the marquess's. It would be a sensible business partnership.

From downstairs came the strains of a waltz. Felicity felt a tremor of excitement and ran to the long looking-glass in her room and twisted this way and that to make sure the tapes of her gown were correctly tied.

"'Bout time you started to care for your looks, my lady," grumbled Wanstead.

"Must you always be complaining?" snapped Felicity, colouring up.

There was a scratching at the door. Wanstead opened it. The footman with the branch of candles. Time for Felicity's grand entrance.

Felicity walked out and along the corridor, followed by the footman. Behind the footman came Wanstead, calling out, "Short steps, my lady. Do not stride along like that. Mince, my lady. Mince!"

At the top of the double staircase, Felicity paused and looked down. Faces were turned up to her: her mother's, pale and anxious; her father's, florid and amused. And then she saw the Marquess of Ravenswood. He was very handsome indeed, thought Felicity with a little stab of shock. She had not had a chance to see him in evening dress before. He had thick fair hair cut in a fashionable Brutus crop, a strong body, broad shoulders and slim hips and fine legs, all in the glory of Weston's tailoring. His arrogant high-nosed face briefly turned up to where Felicity stood. Beside him was a beautiful diminutive blonde, all in pink. The marquess glanced up at Felicity with a look of amused contempt and then turned back to his companion, who was laughing up at him.

Felicity thought the marquess's glance of contempt was because she looked like a guy. Her pleasure in her appearance fled. She felt gawky and clumsy. The fact that the marquess might have heard of all her exploits and had taken her in dislike did not cross her mind. She felt it was just like that awful time when she had put on that pretty gown and her father had sneered at her. All of this took but a moment.

Felicity swung a leg over the polished banister and slid down the staircase, vaulted over the polished carved heraldic beast on the bottom post and landed lightly in the hall, to cries of shock from the ladies and roars of noisy approval from the hunting crowd.

The evening was a nightmare for Lady Baronsheath.

Not once did the marquess ask Felicity to dance. He was flirting with Miss Betty Andrews, the lady in pink. He took Miss Andrews in to supper, while Felicity was partnered by Tommy Lush, a hard-swearing, hard-drinking vicar who appeared to have forgotten that his wife was present.

Felicity drank too much at supper. Her eyes were glittering and her thin cheeks flushed. She appeared to be having a marvellous time. It would have eased Lady Baronsheath's distress had she known her daughter was feeling bewildered and miserable, but she did not. Felicity's behaviour was so like the earl's, the earl who was bawling with laughter and slapping everyone on the back and telling warm stories.

The earl was to set out on the first stage of his journey to America in the morning. Lady Baronsheath would be left behind with the horrendous job of preparing Felicity for her London Season. She had prayed that Ravenswood might propose, that *anyone* might propose, so as to make such an ordeal unnecessary. But now she would have to go through with it.

It was when a half-drunk Felicity started whooping her way like a Highland savage through a Scottish reel that Lady Baronsheath slipped away to the drawing-room and took out the crumpled newspaper and smoothed out that advertisement. She sat down and began to write. One of the grooms would start out for London that very evening. Lady Baronsheath felt she needed all the help she could get.

❧ ❧

Amy was down in the dark pit of the kitchen, toasting cheese, when the letter arrived. A round of Cheshire cheese had been Mr. Haddon's latest present. It had arrived two days before, and already Amy and Effy were sick of cheese but felt, for reasons of economy, that they must try to eat it all.

She heard the drawing-room bell jangle and looked up in irritation at the row of black bells on their wires over the kitchen door.

It was typical of Effy to go on as if they still had a house full of servants.

Amy climbed the stairs slowly. She was feeling very tired and her back hurt. That morning, when she had looked in her glass, she had found two large crow's-feet stamped on the puffy flesh under her eyes. Amy needed spectacles, but felt that the getting of them would under- line her age, and so she had sat up reading the night before, squinting at the pages of a romance by the light of one tallow candle. Hence the crow's-feet.

Effy was sitting before a blazing fire in the drawing room, attired in the thinnest of muslins.

"I can see your garters," growled Amy, slumping into a chair opposite. "Christ! I'm tired."

"Language! Language!" admonished Effy.

"Slut on ye," said Amy with a massive shrug. "What's in the letter?"

"The shop kindly sent it round to us because they had a delivery to make in Oxford Street hard by. It is from the Countess of Baronsheath. She needs help in the bringing out of her daughter, Lady Felicity Vane."

"Huzza!" cried Amy, kicking her big feet up into the air. "Why are you not overcome with delight, Effy?"

"Because her ladyship summons us to Sussex, to Greenboys House."

"Then we must set out," cried Amy. "This very day!"

"But it is in the *country*," wailed Effy.

Effy hated the country with a passion. Streatham, with its promise of riches to come, had just been bearable. But Sussex was the *real* country, with trees and grass and birds

22

and all those other weird things. The country to Effy meant social failure. Life was in London, London was the centre of the universe; the country was hell.

"You will have to be brave," said Amy. "We are going to a stately home, not a shepherd's hut. How much money should we demand? She will need to pay us something in advance. And think of the advantages! Lady Baronsheath will not be interviewing us *here!*"

"I feel a spasm coming on," said Effy faintly. She gave a strangled noise and toppled out of her chair onto the floor.

Amy got up and twitched the letter out of her sister's hands, then sat down and began to read it carefully. Effy sat up, looking outraged.

"How can you be so heartless, Amy?"

"Umm," said Amy, still reading. Then she looked up. "You'd better go and change into something decent, Effy. No need to look like a tart."

"I do *not* look like a tart!"

"Yes, you do. Your garters are made of pink wool, and the knitting in the right one is cobbled. And you haven't any drawers on."

"The wearing of drawers is a masculine fashion."

"Not any more, it ain't," said Amy. "Besides, you'll freeze to death."

"Perhaps we should consult my dear Mr. Haddon," ventured Effy.

"*Our* dear Mr. Haddon," said Amy furiously. "No time. Do stop maundering and mopping and mowing because you're frightened a tree will up and rape you."

"Amy!"

"Get along, do," said Amy, and marched off to book a post-chaise, determined to charge the countess for the cost of it should their services be refused.

Unaware that fate in the shape of the Tribble sisters was bearing down on her, Felicity rode out on a still November morning two weeks after the ball. It was unusually mild for the time of year. The air was full of the smell of wood-smoke and the winy tang of rotten leaves. She was alone. Her father had never insisted that a groom should accompany her, and although the earl had left, Felicity saw no reason to change the freedom of her ways. Her mother had been unusually quiet and abstracted and had not even chided her for her behaviour at the ball.

But in the past few days, Felicity had begun to wonder what the future held for her. With her adored father gone, the desire to please him by drinking, roistering, shooting, and hunting had left her. She preferred to be alone. It had been raining for days and the ground was heavy and soggy. The trunks of the tall trees glittered with green mould, and only a few red and yellow leaves still clung to their branches.

Her mare, Titbit, clopped along the country lanes, as content as her mistress to wander slowly and aimlessly. The trees which had arched overhead gave way to brown fields bordered by thorn hedges and then to open heathland.

At the top of a rise was a man on a horse. Felicity recognized the Marquess of Ravenswood. He was dressed in a pink hunting coat, leather breeches, and boots with mahogany tops. He wore an old-fashioned three-cornered hat on his head.

Felicity raised her riding crop in salute. He touched his hat, and then, spurring his horse, set off away from her as fast as he could.

"Damn him," muttered Felicity. "If he prefers little

sugarplums like Miss Betty Andrews, he is not the man for me." But a nasty little voice seemed to be trying to tell her that the taste of all gentlemen was for fluffy little blondes. At the ball, her cronies of the hunting field had treated her like another man, and a few had even forgotten themselves enough to confide in her their hopeless passion for Miss This or Miss That.

The marquess had ridden off, more because he wanted to be alone than because he particularly wanted to avoid the company of Lady Felicity Vane. He had no strong feelings about the girl. He had a certain warm sympathy for the plight of her mother being cursed with such a wayward daughter, and a contempt for girls who behaved like men. He wanted to think about Miss Betty Andrews and to wonder again whether she would make a suitable wife.

The fact that she did not have much in her brain-box did not worry him greatly. He wanted an attractive, compliant wife and several sons and daughters. Miss Andrews had a round bottom and generous hips. She would probably breed well. The marquess might have viewed his intended less like a farmer looking over a cow at market had he ever been in love, but he had not. Not even in his adolescence had anything other than lust troubled his life. He regarded books and poems about romantic love as a form of necessary sophistication, to give a polite varnish to baser feelings.

The lowing of cattle, mixed with the shrill sounds of someone screaming, interrupted his reverie. He rode to the top of a small hill which overlooked the Lewes Road and looked down.

A herd of cows was ambling slowly past a dusty post-chaise. In the chaise was a little lady, screaming like a banshee through the open window, while a tall companion tried to soothe her. The cowherd was grinning and deliberately not trying to make the herd move any faster.

The marquess rode down to the road, dismounted, tethered his horse and began to wave his hat to shoo the cows into a faster pace. The cowherd, recognizing the marquess, moved the herd along as well, and soon the post-chaise was left on the clear road.

The marquess went up to the carriage on the tall woman's side and made a low bow. She jerked down the glass.

"Thank you," she said gruffly. "That pox of a yokel would have kept us here all day and my sister is in hysterics. Oh, do shut up, Effy. The bloody things have gone and here is a Sir Galahad, come to rescue you."

The sobbing stopped and a pretty lady with white hair appeared beside the tall one.

"Thank you, sir," she said. "You are so brave."

The marquess looked amused. "I did not rescue you from footpads, ma'am. Merely from a herd of cows. I am Ravenswood."

"And I am Miss Amy Tribble," said the tall woman, "and this here is my sister, Effy Tribble."

"*Miss* Effy," said the other faintly. "You must forgive my sister, my lord. Her speech is very plain." Effy knew the names of all the peerage.

"Can you give our silly Jehu the direction of the nearest inn?" asked Amy. "We are bound for the Baronsheaths but do not want to arrive in our dirt."

"My home is quite near," said the marquess. "If you would care to follow me, I would be glad to entertain you and send a man over to Greenboys with the intelligence of your arrival."

"So kind," said Effy, batting her lamp-blackened eyelashes at him. The marquess fought down an unmanly

26

desire to giggle. How old were these ladies? Fifty or so, surely. And yet the white-haired one was flirting outrageously.

He told the driver of the post-chaise to follow him, remounted, and set off in the direction of his home, Ansley Court.

Soon the Tribble sisters found themselves ushered into a bedchamber where they could wash and change before travelling on to Greenboys.

As soon as they were alone, Amy rounded on Effy. "How could you be so wanton?" she cried. "Flirting and ogling like a very strumpet. You are old enough to be his mother."

"He is in his thirties," said Effy defiantly.

"Still too young for you."

Effy began to cry. Amy looked at her impatiently and then her face softened. She had bullied and bullied to get Effy down into the dreaded country. Enough was enough. "I am truly sorry," said Amy, hugging her sobbing sister, "but you must see how important Ravenswood is to our plans."

Effy dried her eyes. "No, I don't see," she said huffily.

"He is unmarried," said Amy, "and our job is to find a suitor for this Lady Felicity. Let us sound him out and find out if he has any tender feelings for the girl."

Changed and washed, the Tribbles were soon sitting in the library in front of the fire, being refreshed with ratafia and macaroon biscuits.

"We are looking forward to meeting Lady Felicity," said Amy. "A charming girl, I believe."

The marquess said nothing.

"I said she is a charming girl," said Amy very loudly.

The marquess winced. "I am not deaf, Miss Amy."

"Well, my lord?"

"Well, what?" he demanded impatiently.

Amy cleared her throat and tried again. "What is your opinion of Lady Felicity?"

"I thought I was making it plain I did not want to voice an opinion."

"Why?" demanded Amy with the stubbornness of a child.

"Do not go on so, dear sister," interrupted Effy. "We are understandably anxious to know as much as possible about this job before—"

She broke off in confusion as Amy glared at her.

"Job?" The marquess looked surprised. "Are you joint governesses or something of that nature?"

The look of frozen hauteur on Effy's face made him colour slightly.

"My lord, I would have you know we are chaperones extraordinary," said Effy. "We could not possibly be governesses. We are the Wiltshire Tribbles. We are bon ton. Our job is to bring Lady Felicity out."

"Is Lady Baronsheath unwell?" asked the marquess.

"No, my lord," said Effy stiffly. She had still not forgiven him for thinking they might be governesses. "Her ladyship is in need of our special services."

"Those being?"

"We make the best of the worst," said Amy.

"What an exhausting profession," said the marquess, thinking of Felicity.

"This is our first job," said Amy bluntly, "and we need all the help we can get."

The marquess thought ruefully of all the stories he had heard about Lady Felicity since he had returned from abroad. His neighbours had told him that she had been disgracefully behaved from the time she could first walk and had routed several nurses and governesses.

"I have some business which takes me to Town," he said slowly. He had taken a liking to these two odd sisters.

28

He noticed the faded and shabby grandeur of their old-fashioned clothes. Effy's one modern gown, the transparent muslin, had been hidden before departure by Amy. "Perhaps if you can send me word when you intend to return, I could escort you. I have a very comfortable travelling carriage."

Effy leaned forward and rapped him playfully on the knuckles with her fan. "We are most grateful to you, my lord," she said. "The terrors of the countryside would appear as nothing in your company."

"What terrors, Miss Effy?"

Effy shuddered. "Oh, fields and cows and bulls and birds and trees and all that sort of thing. So undisciplined! So threatening! There is just too much of it."

"But what of London with its footpads and badly lit streets and almost constant smell of sewage?" asked the marquess.

Effy turned pink and frowned. The marquess, she thought, was almost as distressingly plain-spoken as her sister. Talking to a gently bred lady about sewage. Fie!

"London is the centre of elegance and wit," she said disapprovingly. "Perhaps the difficulty with Lady Felicity—if there is any difficulty—is that the poor girl has been too long in unrefined surroundings. The country is a monstrous coarsening sort of place."

"Perhaps," said the marquess. "And yet it does not seem to have had a destructive effect on the manners of any of our other local belles. In truth, Lady Felicity is a spoilt brat."

"I am sure you are overharsh," said Amy hopefully.

"We shall see. Now, if you are ready, ladies, we shall be on our way."

Felicity had been told of her mother's plans for her that morning. She had been highly amused. The Tribble sisters

would soon be routed just like that long line of governesses and nurses. She was, however, prepared to offer
them a courteous welcome until she made up her mind
how best to be shot of them.

But the Tribbles, having paid off their post-chaise, arrived in the Marquess of Ravenswood's carriage. The
marquess himself courteously helped them to alight before driving off. All this, Felicity saw from her bedroom
window.

Felicity smarted with humiliation. That *he* of all people
should know her mother considered her so unruly that
she had sent for help made her burn with rage.

Lady Baronsheath received the Tribbles in her drawing-room. She was taken aback by their appearance. Miss
Effy was all that was genteel, but the swansdown trim of
her pelisse was yellowish and ragged and there was a neat
darn in one of the elbows of her gown. Miss Amy had
divested herself of her balding fur cloak to reveal a dingy
brown round gown with the waist in the wrong place.
Neither lady appeared to possess one scrap of jewellery.

For their part, the Tribbles were delighted with the
countess. She was well-bred and quiet with a charming,
if diffident, manner. Both were beginning to entertain
high hopes of Felicity.

Lady Baronsheath questioned them closely as to their
friends and connections and looked happier as she recognized the names of several of her own friends.

"My daughter," said Lady Baronsheath, "is wayward
and spoilt, but I know that, *au fond,* she has a good heart.
She has not had much in the way of religious training.
Our vicar, Mr. Simms, is a very good man, but quite
timid, and I am afraid his little talks with Felicity do not
seem to have done any good at all."

"Don't worry, my lady," said Amy gruffly. "Lady Felicity shall read her Bible every night and every morning."

The countess blinked. "Well, well, perhaps that might help, if by any chance you can get her to obey you."

"Oh, Lady Felicity will obey me," said Amy. "Or else."

That was when Lady Baronsheath began to regret the whole thing. Amy looked so tall, so strong, so eccentric, and so menacing, that she feared her poor Felicity would be ill-treated. The Tribbles' fate hung in the balance. Then Lady Baronsheath decided to send them packing.

She half-rose to her feet. Her mouth opened to issue the dismissal, when Effy said, "So kind of Lord Ravenswood to offer to escort us to London when we depart with Lady Felicity."

Lady Baronsheath sat down again. "Ravenswood! Are you sure?"

"Yes," said Effy innocently. "He bravely rescued us from a herd of charging bulls—"

"Cows! Cows!" put in Amy.

"Bulls," said Effy firmly. "And then he took us to his home so we might change into our best before we met you, Lady Baronsheath. When he heard we were to take Lady Felicity to London, he offered his services as escort."

Lady Baronsheath worried only briefly over Effy's artless remark about changing into their best clothes. If those are their best, she thought, what on earth are the second-best ones like? But Ravenswood! Surely his offer to accompany them showed he must have some feeling for Felicity.

"You shall meet my daughter now," said Lady Baronsheath.

She walked over to where an embroidered bell-pull hung beside the fireplace and gave it a firm tug.

Chapter 3

Poh! did ever one see such a troublesome bear?
No, I will not get up from my seat now, I
swear.
Lord! what can you mean by this pulling and
teasing?
Sure, there's nothing so bad as a man without
reason!
Delia Very Angry *(Anonymous)*

FELICITY WALKED INTO THE room and dropped a full court curtsy, her eyes dancing with laughter. She thought the Tribble sisters were the funniest pair of eccentrics she had ever seen.

Introductions were made by Lady Baronsheath. Amy and Effy studied Felicity closely. Both were initially relieved to find the girl passably attractive. A squint or a stoop would have been a definite drawback. Felicity sat down and assumed a demure air. Her mother knew that look and knew her daughter was planning mischief.

"The Misses Tribbles are to prepare you for the Season, Felicity," said Lady Baronsheath. "You will go with them to London and there will learn the arts of being a fashionable lady."

"I do not need schooling," said Felicity quietly. "I know very well how to go on."

"Then why don't you?" demanded Amy.

Lady Baronsheath's hands made a fluttering, useless motion of protest. Felicity's eyes narrowed.

"Why don't I *what?*"

"Go on like a fashionable young lady?" said Amy equably.

"I behave according to my rank and breeding," said Felicity, her eyes lingering deliberately on Amy's shabby gown.

"Fancy!" said Amy. "One would never have guessed."

Felicity conjured up a weary sigh. "Mama, are you going to sit there and see me insulted by these persons?"

"There you are!" said Amy triumphantly, before Lady Baronsheath could speak. "Now that was a crass piece of rudeness. In future you will address me as Miss Amy and my sister as Miss Effy."

"When do we set out for London?" asked Felicity, quickly making up her mind to deal with these two frights once she was out of her mother's sight.

Amy looked around the comfortable room, at the bowls of hothouse flowers, at the cheerful crackle of the fire, and said firmly, "Tomorrow."

"Tomorrow!" wailed Effy. "We are but arrived, dear sister, and I am monstrous fatigued from the journey. Besides, dear Lord Ravenswood will not be able to accompany us at such short notice."

"Ravenswood?" demanded Felicity. "What has he to say to the matter?"

"He kindly offered us his escort to London," explained Effy. "Oh, Amy, do not let us be so precipitate. We need a gentleman's protection in this dreadful country."

"We are not overly plagued with highwaymen or foot-pads at the moment," said Felicity, fighting down her fury at the very idea of Ravenswood's escort.

"My dear, the country just *reeks* with trees and birds and bulls and things like that," said Effy helplessly.

Felicity decided that the last thing she wanted was Lord Ravenswood to witness her being taken off to be schooled by these quizzes. She would back Miss Amy, set off for London, and frighten the sisters into getting rid of her.

"Tomorrow suits me very well," she said.

"Leave us, Felicity," said Lady Baronsheath. "I must speak to these ladies in private."

Felicity rose and curtsied and left the room without a backward glance.

"Now," said Lady Baronsheath firmly, "will you please explain the reason for this speedy departure?"

"There's a lot of work to be done, my lady," said Amy, "and from the look in her eye, Lady Felicity plans to be shot of us as soon as she can. I can't begin to discipline her in her family home. If you want the next Season to be a success, the sooner we start the better."

Lady Baronsheath hesitated only a moment—a moment during which she thought of the mayhem Felicity could create. "Very well," she said faintly, ignoring Effy's squawk of protest. "I shall send a note to Lord Ravenswood, telling him the time of your departure, but I fear he will not be able to accompany you at such short notice. But can we discuss this further? I must confess I have doubts . . ."

She was about to say that she was regretting having sent for them. They *were* very odd, and this rushing off so quickly, despite their seemingly reasonable explanation, had nonetheless made her anxious about Felicity's welfare.

It was Effy who innocently secured the Tribble future.

"I would much rather have the marquess's escort," she said wistfully, "but then, it is not as if we shall never see him again. He said he was most eager to call on us when he was resident in London."

Lady Baronsheath looked at the two sisters. Was it possible they could effect a change in Felicity? Was it possible they could even make Ravenswood propose? She thought of coping with her daughter herself, and shuddered.

"We have not discussed terms," she said.

Amy opened the drawstrings of a reticule that looked like a poacher's bag and fished out a notebook. But before she could say anything, Effy leaned forward. "You must appreciate, my lady," she said, "the vast expense of the routs and dinners we must hold, not to mention the hiring of a dancing master, music teacher, and water-colourist. I suggest you pay us the necessary sum in advance on the understanding that, should the experiment fail, such money as has not been used will be returned to you. I suggest we give you a letter promising that fact. Then, should Felicity be engaged by the end of the Season to a suitable gentleman, a bonus would be in order."

"How much?" asked Lady Baronsheath.

Amy eagerly flipped open the pages of her notebook. She planned to surprise Lady Baronsheath with the modesty of their demands.

"Eight thousand pounds," said Effy quietly.

Amy's mouth fell open.

Lady Baronsheath thought quickly. Instead of being daunted by the sum, she was strangely reassured. The best of everything always cost the most.

"Very well," she said. "I will give you a draft."

Amy turned bright red.

"And now, if you will excuse me, ladies," said the countess, rising to her feet. "I must tell the maid to prepare Felicity for her journey and also apprise Lord Ravenswood of your departure."

Both sisters rose as well and curtsied.

Felicity, who had been marching angrily about the lawns, stopped outside the long drawing-room windows and looked in. An amazing sight met her eyes. The sisters were capering about the room, doing a mad jig.

They are quite crazy, she thought in amazement. I shall be shot of them before we even reach London!

Felicity was very quiet as Lord Ravenswood's travelling carriage set out on the long road to London. The parting from her mother had upset her more than she would have believed possible. Her whole young life had been one drive to please her father, and somewhere along the way her gentle mother had been largely forgotten. It finally sank into Felicity's mind that her mother had been very deeply troubled indeed to send her only daughter out to be schooled by strangers.

She was intimidated by the presence of the marquess, who was travelling inside with them. Somewhere deep inside, he seemed to be laughing at her.

Miss Effy had promptly fallen asleep as soon as the carriage set out, and Miss Amy, after exchanging a few pleasantries with the marquess, had followed suit. Both sisters were exhausted after a sleepless night of elation. Felicity turned her profile to the marquess, who was sitting opposite and looked out of the window. A thick blanket of fog had rolled in from the Channel to blot out the Sussex Downs, the chalky Downs where she had recently ridden, free as a bird.

The carriage moved inexorably on, through tiny villages of flintstone houses, water from the thick mist dripping from the thatch. Behind came a fourgon, laden with Felicity's trunks and guarded by her lady's maid.

The marquess studied the averted face opposite. He reflected lazily that Lady Felicity had a certain attraction when she was as modishly dressed as she was for the journey. She was wearing a habit of dark-green Georgian cloth, ornamented with military frogs. On her head was a dashing hat of green velvet trimmed with white fur. It was tilted rakishly to one side, exposing a cluster of glossy curls. He opened his mouth to enter into conversation with her, thought the better of it, took a book from his pocket and began to read.

Immediately aware his attention was elsewhere, Felicity turned and looked at him, and then down at the book on his lap. He was leaning forward with his chin on his hand. Greek! The book was written in ancient Greek.

"I don't believe you can read a word of that," said Felicity crossly. "You are simply trying to impress me."

"No, Lady Felicity, I am not trying to impress you," he said, without raising his eyes from the page. "In fact, I cannot envisage any future time where I should want to do anything at all to capture your attention."

Felicity flushed angrily and bit back a retort. Unbidden, a sharp memory of her coming-out ball came to her mind. Before that ball, she had enjoyed her easy popularity with the gentlemen of the county, particularly the gentlemen of the hunt. It had been forcibly borne in on her at that dance that her father's training had worked all too well. Despite her ballgown and elegant coiffure, they had almost regarded her as another man. Jack Dempster, her companion of the hunting field, had been quite white with emotion after a dance with Miss Betty Andrews and had confided in Felicity that if Miss Andrews did not smile on him but once, he would go and shoot himself. No man had sighed or trembled under *her* gaze. For the first time in her young life, Felicity longed for some of that magic feminine power that could make strong men weak.

They broke their journey at a posting inn for some refreshment. Felicity would have liked a glass of wine, but Effy quietly ordered lemonade for the ladies. As they journeyed on again, Felicity began to hate her companions. The marquess's sheer indifference to her was galling. She detested the Tribble sisters. She became sure her mother had been tricked by them. Such a shabby pair could not possibly have the correct entrée to the polite saloons of London.

They stopped at six o'clock in the evening at another posting house to rack up for the night. It was built on the old plan with the bedrooms leading off wooden galleries overlooking a square courtyard.

The marquess was supervising the stabling of the horses and the Tribble sisters were leading the way up one of the wooden staircases to the bedrooms, with Felicity following behind, when Felicity dropped her reticule. Before she could stoop to retrieve it, a gentleman darted forward and picked it up for her. Felicity was about to thank him in her usual free and frank manner when she remembered Miss Betty Andrews. Some imp made her lower her eyelashes and glance up at the gentleman from under them as she took her reticule from him. She murmured a shy "Thank you." He was a tall, athletic young man of her own age with a mop of thick black curls. With a dawning new feeling of power, she noticed the glow in his eyes.

"Do you travel to London, Miss . . . ?" he asked.

"Lady Felicity Vane," whispered Felicity. "And you are . . . ?"

"Bremmer. James Bremmer."

"I thank you, Mr. Bremmer. I am fearfully clumsy."

"Lord Bremmer, Lady Felicity."

"Yes, Lord Bremmer, I go to London to be prepared for a Season."

"May I say, Lady Felicity, in my opinion you need no preparation whatsoever."

Felicity simpered. "La, sir, you are too bold."

"Forgive me. Your beauty has made me bold. Do you dine this evening?"

"Yes, my lord, my chaperones keep London hours and I have not yet eaten."

"Nor I. Perhaps we shall meet . . ."

"I think not, Bremmer," said a cold voice. "I have bespoke a private parlour. To your room, Lady Felicity."

The Marquess of Ravenswood stood there, his handsome face dark with displeasure.

To his surprise, Felicity cast him a scared look and then an appealing one in the direction of Lord Bremmer, before picking up her skirts and scurrying up the stairs. She raised her skirts too high, showing Lord Bremmer and the marquess that Lady Felicity Vane had a well-turned ankle.

Lord Bremmer flushed angrily. "What is the meaning of this, Ravenswood?" he demanded. "You go on like a tyrant. Is Lady Felicity your niece?"

"No," said the marquess curtly. "I happen to be escorting her and her chaperones to London. The Tribble sisters."

"The Tribbles!" exclaimed Lord Bremmer. "I thought I recognized them. What are two of London's most eccentric eccentrics doing chaperoning such a delicate and beautiful lady?"

"Bremmer," sighed the marquess. "Mind your own business."

Felicity had been looking forward to the prospect of enslaving Lord Bremmer further at dinner. She was, therefore, most disappointed to find out that the arrangement for the private parlour still held and picked at her food in sulky silence.

The marquess apologized for the paucity of the fare and suggested ordering something else, but the Tribbles said happily there was more than enough. Dinner consisted of beans and bacon, a roasted chine of mutton, giblet pie, hashed goose, and a roasted rabbit with peas, followed by tarts, puddings, and jellies.

The Tribbles ate in a steady, preoccupied silence. At one point, Amy opened the strings of her reticule and cast a furtive look at the marquess. Felicity yelped in surprise as Effy kicked her under the table in mistake for Amy. Amy looked at Effy, Effy shook her head and smiled, and Amy dropped her reticule to the floor. Felicity wondered what the pantomime meant. Amy had, in fact, been wondering whether to hide some of the food in her reticule and had been stopped by Effy. Amy was the one who could not believe their luck and dreaded a return to the days of insufficient food.

The marquess then began to talk to them about various people in Town whom Felicity did not know. She wondered whether to flirt with the marquess to see the effect, but one look at his hard and handsome face persuaded her it would be a waste of time.

Finally, she begged to be excused. When she left, she stood outside the door and listened.

"Oof!" she heard Amy exclaim. "Peace at last. May we

take wine with you, my lord? I confess that all this lemonade is making me feel bilious, but Lady Felicity has too much of a fondness for strong drink for a girl of her age."

"By all means," Felicity heard the marquess say in an amused voice. There came a gurgling of wine being poured, and then the marquess's voice again. "To your success, ladies," he said, "and may you find Lady Felicity a husband. It should not be too difficult. There will be plenty of gentlemen prepared to overlook her gaucherie for the sake of her dowry."

Felicity walked angrily away. And so she did not hear Amy's gruff reply. "You are too hard on the child, Ravenswood. She simply needs some Town bronze. She is not precisely beautiful by fashionable standards, but, bless me, she has a figure like a Greek goddess, which is, to my mind, far more appealing than these roly-poly dimpled misses you gentlemen swoon over."

The night was clear and frosty, and Felicity stopped outside the door of her room and leaned her elbows on the wooden rail of the gallery and looked down into the courtyard. There was a young man strolling up and down, smoking a cheroot. Lord Bremmer.

Felicity dived into her room, soaked her handkerchief in the water jug, and returned to the balcony. As the young man walked below her, she squeezed the handkerchief. A drop of moisture fell on Lord Bremmer's hand. He looked up. Felicity gave a choked sob.

He could see her in the moonlight. She was wearing a white muslin gown and had a richly coloured Norwich shawl about her shoulders.

"Lady Felicity," he called softly. "Why do you cry?"

"Oh, sir," said Felicity in a choked voice. "What is to become of me?"

Lord Bremmer mounted swiftly up the stairs. "What has happened?" he cried.

"Shhh!" said Felicity. "If they find you here, they will beat me."

"Who? Ravenswood?"

"No, the Tribbles."

"This is monstrous. What are your parents about to send you off in such company?"

"My father has gone to America," said Felicity, "and Mama is not strong. These wicked women advertised themselves as chaperones in the newspaper and Mama was quite gulled by them. They say I must marry the first man who asks me, for Mama is to pay them well if I am engaged before the Season is over."

"I shall ride to your home and tell your mother of your plight," said Lord Bremmer.

Felicity looked at him with a certain amount of irritation. He was supposed to propose to her, so that she might know that her new act worked well.

"Alas, she would not believe you," said Felicity with another pathetic sob.

"Then," he said, striking his chest and tossing back his curls in a way that Byron would have envied, "I shall marry you myself!"

Felicity swayed towards him like a sapling in the breeze. "You are too kind, so very kind," she said in a choked voice. "But Ravenswood is in league with them. He wants me for himself, and even Mama says it is her heart's desire that I should marry Ravenswood."

"But why does he want to marry you? He does not seem to look on you with affection."

"Ravenswood has recently lost all his money on 'Change," said Felicity, ever inventive. "I am very rich, you see."

There came the sound of the marquess's voice raised in farewell. "Goodbye . . . forever," breathed Felicity, and she fled to her room and collapsed face down on the bed, giggling. The beginnings of an absolutely splendid plan were beginning to form in her head. She was still giggling helplessly when Wanstead came in to prepare her for bed.

The Tribble sisters were beginning to feel more and more apprehensive as London drew nearer. They felt they would be starting at a disadvantage when Lady Felicity found they had not any servants. Amy privately meant to ask the marquess for help. She knew Effy would be shocked at such a suggestion and planned somehow to see the marquess on his own. They stopped again at another posting house. Both sisters were now too worried to notice the strange docility of Lady Felicity.

Dinner was over and still Amy had not found any opportunity for a private talk with the marquess. Sharing a room with her sister, she lay in bed and read and read until gentle snoring told her Effy was asleep. Amy rose and dressed and made her way quietly along to the marquess's room and scratched on the door.

There was a surprised "Enter." Heart beating hard, Amy pushed open the door and went in. The marquess was lying in bed, a book on his lap.

"Miss Amy!" he cried. "Is something wrong?"

"I need your help, my lord," said Amy, carrying a chair over to the bed and sitting down. "The fact is, we have no servants."

"None at all? No lady's maid. No . . . ?"

"Nothing," said Amy, flapping her large feet up and down in embarrassment. "We now have enough of the ready from Lady Baronsheath to hire the lot, but it will look bad when we arrive with Lady Felicity and she finds an empty house. We cannot discipline the child and we do not gain her respect."

The marquess lifted his dressing-gown from the end of the bed and put it on. "Let us sit by the fire, Miss Amy," he said, "and try to decide what is best. You could always say it was the servants' day off."

"Yes, but she would see us interviewing servants on the following days, and she will think we are tricksters who have taken her mother's money on false pretences."

The marquess's face cleared. "I will send one of my men ahead to my Town house and tell him to move my staff to your home for the first week. You must let me have the key to your house."

Amy opened her reticule and emptied it out on the floor in front of her. There was an odd assortment of pins and books, knitting, an enormous key, and a half-eaten pie. "Don't know how that got there," said Amy, blushing and stuffing the pie out of sight again. She handed him the key. "My lord," said Amy solemnly, "you are an angel."

"I am only helping to set you up in business." He laughed. "Go to bed, Miss Amy, and leave everything to me."

Felicity had been out walking in the posting-house garden. She had hoped Lord Bremmer might have followed them, but there was no sign of him. She was returning to her room when the door of the marquess's room opened. Felicity drew back into the shadows, not wanting him to see her.

As she watched, Miss Amy came out looking flushed and happy. She was followed by the marquess, wearing his dressing-gown.

"Your price is above pearls, my dear Miss Amy," said the marquess. He raised Amy's hand to his lips and kissed it.

Felicity began to tremble. Disgusting! She had heard

whispers of the decadent behaviour of certain London gentlemen. He had been entertaining that old fright in his bedchamber, and Felicity was sure "entertaining" was too polite a word.

Hot tears ran down her cheeks. The Tribbles deserved every shame she could bring on them.

On the remainder of the journey to London, the Marquess of Ravenswood's interest in Lady Felicity Vane was at last aroused. He found her attitude to him most odd. When he took her hand to help her enter or alight from the carriage, her whole body seemed to shrink from him, and her wide startled eyes were always quickly veiled by her lashes, but not before he surprised a look of disgust in them. From treating her casually like a naughty and rather tiresome schoolgirl, he set himself to please. But she replied in monosyllables and then seemed to spend a great deal of time pretending to be asleep.

It was when they broke their journey for the last time outside London that Amy decided to take matters in hand. She and Effy had been alarmed at Felicity's cringing air. Each nourished hopes of startling and amazing Lady Baronsheath by presenting the Marquess of Ravenswood as a son-in-law. Now the marquess was showing a very pretty interest in the girl, Felicity must needs spoil it by near-fainting with disgust every time she looked at him.

The sisters conferred in the room that had been reserved for them to wash and rest in before continuing on the last stage of the journey.

"Perhaps I have the more delicate touch, Amy dear," said Effy. "You have too robust a manner to broach such a tender subject."

"And I think it should be left to me," said Amy, striding up and down and waving her arms like a windmill. "For I, too, am a subject of her disgust and I want to know why. You are not plain-spoken enough, Effy, and you will hint and hint and never get anywhere."

Effy appeared to remain adamant, and it was only after Amy swore most terribly and said that if they could not agree, then she would have to ask Ravenswood himself to deal with the matter, that Effy caved in.

Effy went off to fetch Felicity, who at last entered and stood near the doorway, her eyes lowered.

"Now, let's have it," said Amy, after her sister had reluctantly left. "What is the reason for your scarcely veiled hatred of me?"

"I am bound to dislike two strangers who have set themselves up as my mentors and are, in my opinion, ill-qualified for the job," said Felicity icily.

Amy's temper broke. "Christ and slut on ye," she roared. "We were not so mealy-mouthed in my generation. It is not only I who suffer from your dumb insolence but Ravenswood, too. Speak out, or are you as gutless as you look at this moment?"

Colour flooded into Felicity's white cheeks and she clenched her fists. "How dare you lecture me, you old trollop," she hissed. "I saw you with my own eyes, coming out of Ravenswood's bedchamber and he in his undress and kissing your hand. Pah!"

Amy stared at her in amazement, and then she began to laugh. She roared with laughter and slapped her thigh. At last she choked out, "Bedamned. If that ain't the biggest compliment I have ever had in my life. Me, Amy Tribble—a light-skirt! Fie, for shame. I went to ask Ravenswood a favour. Don't you see, you goose, that only a lady of my looks and age can safely visit a man in his bedchamber? Ravenswood! He, who could have any female in the land. What does he want to bed an old warhorse like me for? Hey?"

"Oh, dear," said Felicity, ludicrous in her dismay. She was furious with Amy for having made her feel like a fool, but her sense of the ridiculous got the better of her and she began to giggle helplessly.

"That's better," said Amy, surveying her with satisfaction. "I tell you, Lady Felicity, had I not been able to laugh at some of life's problems, I would ha' been in my grave this while since."

Felicity felt a rush of affection for the odd Amy which she quickly stifled. The Tribbles must be punished for having taken her away from home. But somehow, the light, happy feeling persisted and the marquess later was rewarded with a blinding smile as he helped her into the carriage.

He raised his thin eyebrows in surprise. "If you go on smiling like that, Lady Felicity," he said, "then no gentleman in London will be safe from you."

There was an almost festive air about the party now as they rolled towards London.

A light snow had begun to fall, decorating the sooty black buildings with a sparkling frosting of white. A man standing on his roof was brushing off the snow and it spiralled down in a white column in front of the brightly lit windows of a haberdasher's.

The glowing Aladdin's cave of a confectioner's shone through the darkness: pineapples and plums, peaches and pears, and other exotic hothouse fruit; chocolates and comfits and sugarplums. Then a jeweller's with the soft gleam of silver and sparkling prisms of light from diamonds and rubies.

Two guards in scarlet uniforms rode past the carriage, their mounts curvetting and prancing.

To Felicity, it was all part of an exciting overture. The curtain was about to go up on that most dramatic set piece of all—London Town.

For a little while, she even forgot her plans to run away at the first opportunity.

Chapter 4

So Mary got me to bed, and covered me up
warm.
However, she stole away my garters, that I
might
do myself no harm.
—*Jonathan Swift*

MR. HADDON CAUTIOUSLY APPROACHED the Tribbles' home in Holles Street. He had called a few days before but had been intimidated by the sight of so many liveried servants coming and going. He was frightened to ask if the sisters had returned, for he feared to learn they had sold the house and had gone out of his life.

London was still a strange and bewildering place to him. Even accents and modes of speech had changed. The gentlemen drawled out their words, looking down their noses with their eyes half shut, and the ladies interlarded their conversation with bad French.

His bloodline had always, in the past, been much better

than his fortune. Now that he had returned a wealthy nabob, all doors were open to him. But he knew society regarded him as an odd old stick.

Taking a deep breath, he mounted the shallow steps to the door and hammered firmly on the knocker.

The door was answered by the very epitome of the English butler. His heavy-lidded eyes surveyed Mr. Haddon out of a fat white face shadowed by an enormous white wig. His striped waistcoat was stretched over a generous paunch and his green silk coat had gold shoulder knots. His knee-breeches were tied with gold ribbons and his white silk stockings ended in flat black pumps. His feet were placed in the fifth position and his white-gloved hands held an imaginary tray.

"I am called to see the Misses Tribble," said Mr. Haddon, handing over his card.

The butler inclined his head, took the card by one corner in a gloved hand, and stood aside.

Mr. Haddon stepped into the square hall with its black-and-white-tiled floor. He noticed an elaborate bouquet of hothouse flowers in a vase on a console table. He waited uneasily as the butler slowly mounted the stairs. What had happened? Perhaps Lady Baronsheath had employed them, but no fee could account for this sudden air of luxury emanating from the house. He noticed the wall of the staircase now boasted portraits and yet he was sure they were not of the Tribble family.

The butler returned, slowly and pompously, down the stairs.

"If you will follow me, sir," he said.

Mr. Haddon followed his fat back up the stairs.

The butler held open the door of the drawing-room. "Mr. Benjamin Haddon," he shouted.

Mr. Haddon entered. Effy rose to meet him, both hands held out in welcome.

52

"Tea, Humphrey," she said to the butler.

She waited eagerly until the butler had left, giggling at the surprise on Mr. Haddon's face. He looked about him wonderingly, at the pictures on the walls, at the flowers, at some new and fine pieces of furniture.

"Do come and sit by the fire," said Effy, plumping herself down on a backless sofa in a swirl of shawls. "Your wonderful idea worked, and we are employed to bring out Lady Felicity Vane."

"But the servants!" exclaimed Mr. Haddon.

"I see I must begin at the beginning and tell you all," said Effy. She recounted their adventures, wildly exaggerated—the marquess had rescued them from a herd of savage charging bulls—ending with, "And so here we are, in luxury and comfort. Dear Lord Ravenswood said there was no point in recalling his servants. He said he would use a room here when he was in Town and let his Town house for the Season and that way we would not have to pay anything for his servants until the next Season is over. Most generous."

"But the pictures?"

"Lord Ravenswood's secretary is a most efficient man. He had orders to make our dear home look attractive to Lady Felicity and so he removed furniture, paintings, and ornaments from the marquess's home to here!"

The door opened and the butler came in, followed by two footmen carrying a tea-tray. "Tell Miss Amy that Mr. Haddon is here, and tell Lady Felicity to join us as well as soon as her fittings are over," said Effy grandly.

"Such a fuss," she said to Mr. Haddon. "We are furnishing our charge with a really modish wardrobe, and I must say Amy has been most enterprising. She said Lady Felicity must cut a dash since her looks are not of the kind which are commonly admired. We have been returned but three days, and yet Amy insisted, almost as soon as we had arrived, that we go to King's Cross to look for some undiscovered French dressmaker, that being where the poorer of the French emigrées live. It was all so squalid and I said, 'How shall we find one?' and Amy said, 'Look at the clothes they are wearing.' Most odd. For one would never think poor Amy had an eye for fashion. And yet she saw this young and modish female and asked her where she got her gowns—just like that! You know how outspoken Amy is. And the dear creature said she made them herself. So Amy employed her and brought her back here to stay in residence, for the seamstress did not look strong and Amy said King's Cross was enough to give anyone consumption, the buildings being so damp and rickety." She paused for breath.

"Such a change in your fortunes," marvelled Mr. Haddon. He gave a discreet cough. "How old is this Marquess of Ravenswood?"

"I don't know," said Effy. "Quite mature." Mr. Haddon scowled. "Well, I shall take a guess. About thirty-one, I would say."

Mr. Haddon smiled and helped himself to a caraway cake.

"But such a fuss and bustle," went on Effy. "Amy is like a creature *possessed*, I can assure you. You are lucky to find us quiet. She has been interviewing dancing masters, and water-colourists, and music teachers, for, she said, don't you see, that were Lady Felicity allowed to be too quiet, then she might get into mischief. I said, 'Amy,' I said, 'can you not wait until we get our breath?' But she will go on. Lord Ravenswood is all that is helpful, dear man, and if only he might be smitten with Felicity, then what a success we should be. But she is a leetle spoilt. Well, in truth, *very*, and I put it all down to this rights-for-women nonsense. Lady Felicity was in the way of wearing men's clothes. And with her papa's blessing! Unnatural. And—"

She broke off as the door opened and Amy slouched in. She looked tired.

"That little bitch is wearing me out," she said, pouring a cup of tea. She gulped some of the hot liquid and then slumped down in a wing-chair and grinned at Mr. Haddon. "Good to see you," said Amy. "You must hear all the news."

Amy proceeded to try to tell him their adventures only to find to her fury that Effy had been before her with the story.

"You might have waited," said Amy crossly. "It's not fair, Effy. It's my adventure as much as yours, damme."

"Votre mode de parler est un peu de trop," said Effy.

"Speak English," snapped Amy. "We are at war with the Frogs, and I ain't going to have their precious lingo polluting these walls." She glared at Effy.

"Is Lady Felicity being difficult?" asked Mr. Haddon sympathetically.

"Very," groaned Amy. "Mamselle Yvette—that's the new French dressmaker of whom, I have no doubt, my dear sister has already told you all—is trying to do her work patiently and well, and the wretched Felicity will sigh and fidget in such a way that the pins rain down like the leaves in that place Milton was chuntering on about."

"I am very glad to see you both so well and so successful," said Mr. Haddon. "When I called a few days ago and saw all the grand servants and all the bustle, I feared you had sold up and I would never see you again—my last contact with the old world."

"You wasn't very surprised to find we were still both unwed," said Amy. That was something that had rankled in her bosom. She thought it rather unflattering in a way that Mr. Haddon had not even expected either of them to have secured a husband.

"But I was!" lied Mr. Haddon stoutly. He felt he could not quite explain why he had expected them still to be the same, and still unattached, the only people unchanged in a bewildering new world.

"We are both anxious to have new wardrobes for ourselves," said Effy, with a frown at Amy. Effy maintained the fiction that her unwed state was through choice. "But Yvette is not strong and we do not want to overtax her."

"Where is Ravenswood at the moment?" asked Mr. Haddon.

"He has returned to the country. He says he will drop in on us from time to time. It is most fortunate he has taken us under his wing, for he is all that is fashionable, and his generous and clever handling of our affairs has secured our eternal gratitude," said Effy.

"Did you tell Mr. Haddon that it was *I* who asked Ravenswood to help in the matter of servants?" asked Amy.

"Er . . . no," said Effy.

"No, you wouldn't, would you?" declared Amy. "You was always a one for taking credit for everything."

There was an uncomfortable silence.

The door opened and Lady Felicity came in. Her face was flushed with bad temper and her eyes were sparkling.

Mr. Haddon rose to his feet and made a low bow. He privately thought Lady Felicity was one of the most attractive young ladies he had ever seen, and wondered at Amy for having damned the girl's looks as unfashionable.

"Are your fittings completed?" asked Amy.

"For the moment," said Felicity. "I have had just about as much for one day as I can bear."

"You must not tax Mamselle so much," said Effy quietly. "She is a good girl and works hard."

"She is being paid well, no doubt," said Felicity, and then lowered her eyes before Mr. Haddon's look of shock.

Felicity had been thrown by the apparent magnificence of the Tribble residence. She had fully expected to arrive at some poky house in an undistinguished area. But the house in Holles Street had been quickly restored to some of its former magnificence by the marquess's clever secretary. It was a fairly large house, considering it was not a noble mansion, boasting two reception rooms on the ground floor, a drawing-room, dining-room, morning-room, and saloon on the first, and six bedrooms on the third and fourth, as well as the servants' rooms in the attics.

Her plans to run away had not faded. She was biding her time, sure that young Lord Bremmer would put in an appearance again. She planned to upset the Tribbles' plans by using the young man in some way to shame them.

She was slightly intimidated by Amy's authoritarian manner, and as she sipped tea and listened to the sisters making polite conversation with Mr. Haddon, she wondered how best to start upsetting Amy. She thought of all the tricks she had played in the past to rid herself of unwanted governesses. Suddenly she smiled. The campaign against Amy should start that very evening.

Amy noticed that smile, and her heart sank. She felt sure that some plotted piece of mischief could be the only reason why her young charge was looking happy.

When Mr. Haddon had left, she suggested to Effy that they should exert themselves to train Felicity in more ladylike behaviour, but Effy promptly pleaded the headache and retired to bed. Gloomily, Amy decided to set about the task herself.

"Now, Felicity," said Amy. "Let me see you walk across the room and sit down in that chair over by the fireplace.

Felicity haughtily raised her eyebrows, strode across the room and plumped herself down in the chair.

"No, *no,*" said Amy, exasperated. "You must walk with your head held high and never look at your feet. You must never look at the chair you are about to sit on. You must always subside gracefully into it as if a footman is always there to push it under your bottom."

" 'Bottom' is rude," pointed out Felicity with a grin.

"Enough of your childish nonsense," said Amy. She went over to a glass-fronted bookcase and took out a heavy volume, Boswell's *Life of Samuel Johnson.* "Come here," ordered Amy, "and let me put this on your head."

"Oh, really," said Felicity. "How ridiculous."

"DO AS YOU ARE TOLD!" howled Amy with all the ferocity of a dragoon sergeant-major.

"Oh, very well," said Felicity sulkily. She walked back to the door and Amy placed the book on her head. "Now, walk," ordered Amy.

Felicity walked ramrod-straight across the room and lowered herself gingerly into the chair.

"Better," said Amy. "Now, again, and this time you must bridle."

"Bridle?"

"You know very well what I mean. All society ladies must know how to bridle. Tuck in your chin and look as if you have just seen something nasty, but being a lady, you are not going to say anything about it."

Felicity looked at her tormentor mulishly. Amy stared back, hard-eyed. Felicity decided after some moments that revenge on Amy could wait until that evening. It would be easier all round to do as she was bid for the present.

She balanced the book once more on her head, and looked in fixed disdain straight ahead.

"Too rigid," said Amy. "This time bridle and sway slightly as you walk."

Amy kept her at it for an hour before she was satisfied. But she would not allow Felicity to escape. "I am now going to give you a lecture on good manners," she said. "This does not mean saying 'please' and 'thank you,' it means having consideration of other people's sensitivities, whether you are talking to a lord or a shopkeeper."

In vain did Felicity protest. Amy invented and staged situations from buying silks from a stammering shopkeeper to meeting a boring and deaf dowager. Had Felicity not been so furious, she might have found Amy's acting very funny indeed. But as it was, she found nothing amusing in Amy's behaviour. Felicity obeyed her as best she could while a deep resentment burned inside.

By evening, Amy was feeling exhausted. There was a nagging pain in her back, and pouches of fatigue under her eyes. She dropped into her sister's bedroom to say good night. Effy could only mumble a reply as she lay against her lacy pillows looking like a Gothic nightmare. Her face was covered in a mud pack, her white hair was rolled in clay rollers, and she had a chin-strap wound tightly round her head and under her chin.

Amy went off to her own room, where Baxter was waiting to put her to bed. One of the sisters' very first moves had been to rescue their late aunt's lady's maid from the workhouse.

"Aren't you going to open that?" asked Baxter, as she took the pins out of Amy's hair and began to brush it.

"Open what?" asked Amy sleepily.

"That parcel in the corner. It arrived for you early this evening."

"Oh, James, the footman, told me it was from Mr. Haddon, and I decided not to tell Miss Effy so I would have the pleasure of opening it by myself." Amy yawned.

She rose and went over to where the large square parcel stood, picked up the card on top, and read it.

"Dear Miss Amy," Mr. Haddon had written, "The enclosed is a memento of my stay in India and I would very much like you to have it."

"I hope he didn't send anything to Effy as well," murmured Amy. "She is too damn proprietorial about Mr. Haddon."

She wrenched open the top of the box and then leaped back, her hand to her heart.

Baxter took a look and then screamed and rushed and seized the poker and went to smash the contents of the box.

"No, no," said Amy, grabbing the maid's arm. "It must be stuffed."

Amy lifted it out. It was a stuffed cobra. A malevolent-looking thing with wicked glass eyes.

Baxter put down the poker. "If that ain't the nastiest thing I ever did see," she marvelled. "What's that Haddon doing to send sich a thing to a lady?"

"Mr. Haddon to you," growled Amy. "It's quite clever, really, you know, once one gets over the initial shock. But where can I put it? Put it in the drawing-room and we'll frighten every caller away."

Baxter shuddered. "Why not send it to that Mr. Desmond Callaghan, him that stole my mistress's affections away? Two snakes should get on well together."

"No, I'll keep it," said Amy.

Baxter continued her ministrations, but keeping a wary eye all the time on the stuffed cobra. It was so very lifelike with its gleaming eyes and spread hood.

She turned back the blankets. "Get into bed, Miss

Amy," she said, "and try not to rise at dawn as you usually do or you'll wear yourself to a frazzle.

"Lovely bed," sighed Amy luxuriously. She stretched her large bare feet down under the covers and stiffened, her face a mask of horror.

"What is it?" cried Baxter.

Amy threw back the blankets.

When Lady Felicity made an apple-pie bed, she made it properly. Amy's toes were sunk into a very large apple pie. Juice, broken pieces of pastry, and bits of stewed apple were already staining the sheets.

"I'll kill her," snorted Amy, identifying the culprit without any trouble.

"Who, mum?"

"Felicity. Help me up, Baxter, and clean this bed while I go and murder her."

Felicity lay in bed reading, a little smile curving her lips. She had heard Baxter's earlier scream on seeing the cobra and had assumed it to be the sound of Amy screaming when she found the apple pie. Felicity had plenty of pin money and had slipped out to a pastry cook's that afternoon and bought the biggest apple pie in the shop. Serve the old trout right, thought Felicity. Pity Ravenswood wasn't in residence, or she might have played a trick on him as well. He had barely looked at her and had not even troubled to say goodbye. Felicity thought she knew now the reason for his odd interest in the sisters. The portraits of the Tribbles' ancestors all bore a startling resemblance to the present Marquess of Ravenswood. Therefore it followed he was related to the Tribbles and instead of keeping them in funds had sent them out to work. Felicity had not been let into the secret of the servants. The marquess's servants in Town had a different livery from the ones in the country, and so Felicity assumed they were the Tribbles' household staff.

The romance Felicity was reading was one of the first she had ever opened, her father having a great contempt for all such literature. It was the story of a persecuted heiress who finally managed to flee her captors, aided and abetted by a loyal and brave chambermaid.

But engrossing as the tale was, Felicity's eyes began to droop. She blew out the candle and turned over on her side to go to sleep.

She heard the door open quietly but remained as she was. No doubt it was Amy come to harangue her. Something heavy landed on the foot of the bed and then Felicity heard the bedroom door close again.

She struggled up and lit the bed candle and looked at the foot of the bed.

At first it was like a nightmare. She opened her mouth wide, but only choked little noises of fright came out.

An Indian cobra was reared up at the end of the bed, its hood extended, its glittering eyes boring into her own.

Then she found her voice and screamed and screamed. The door opened, Amy marched in, seized the stuffed cobra and marched out again, and slammed the door. Felicity continued to scream, her face white, her eyes dilated. Servants came running, and then Effy. Felicity screamed louder, not recognizing Effy behind the mud pack but thinking some ghoul had risen from the grave to carry her off to the nether regions.

It took a full half-hour to calm her down, by which time Amy had arrived and was leaning nonchalantly against the doorjamb.

"You've had a nightmare," said Effy, who had briefly retired to remove mud and chin-strap and emerge as herself again. "There are no snakes in London. You have had a bad dream. Have you been drinking again?"

"I have had nothing stronger than lemonade!" said Felicity, anger beginning to replace fear. "Someone has played a vicious and nasty trick on me." Her angry eyes glared at Amy.

"It is your imagination," said Amy. "Good heavens. Who in this household would play such a trick on you? We are all mature people. It is only nasty little girls who play such tricks."

Felicity took a deep breath. So that was it. Amy had retaliated.

Amy finally shooed everyone off to bed and then stood looking at Felicity, her arms crossed.

"You behave like a good little girl in future," said Amy. "D'ye hear? You treat me bad, I treat you worse. You deserve to be horsewhipped. Next time, it'll be a crate of spiders. Good night, dear Lady Felicity. Pleasant dreams."

Felicity lay awake for a long time, shaking with rage. Never had her will been crossed so much before. Never had she been afraid of anyone before.

But now she was afraid of Amy Tribble, and hated her accordingly.

Christmas passed, January came and went, and the Marquess of Ravenswood did not return. Felicity was subdued and obedient. She had one great accomplishment. She played the piano very well, having a natural talent, and because her father had liked her to play to him in the evenings. Remorseful Amy was particularly nice to Felicity, feeling she had given the girl much too bad a fright. But Felicity was watching and waiting and biding her time. Lady Baronsheath had called on two occasions but had turned a deaf ear to Felicity's complaints. The countess was impressed by the house and by the fact that Ravenswood would be using it as a base. Felicity had hoped to convey her misery to her mother by being meek and biddable, but all that did was to ease the countess's worry. Timid and shy herself, Lady Baronsheath thought her wayward daughter was learning sense at last.

One day, when pale sunlight was flooding the London streets and a frisky wind had blown away the winter's fogs, Effy and Amy were sitting in the morning-room, enjoying a brief period of peace and quiet. Felicity was out walking with her maid, Wanstead. Wanstead, in Felicity's terms, had "gone over to the enemy camp," which meant the maid was trusted to see that she did not get into any mischief.

It was then that the butler broke the sisters' temporary peace by announcing Mr. Desmond Callaghan.

"Tell that rat we are not at home," said Amy. "The cheek of the man. To steal Auntie's inheritance from us and then come calling as bold as brass."

Mr. Callaghan was just turning angrily away in the hall when Lady Felicity arrived. He swept her a low bow.

"I am sorry to find the Misses Tribble not at home," he said crossly.

Felicity surveyed him with an imp of mischief dancing in her eyes. She thought Mr. Callaghan the most dandified Fribble she had ever seen, from his enormously high beaver hat to his nipped-in waist and high-heeled boots with fixed spurs. His face was highly painted and his petulant mouth rouged.

"I am sure there must be some mistake," said Felicity sweetly. "The Misses Tribble are most definitely at home. Come and I shall introduce you myself." And ignoring the butler's outraged stare, she led the way upstairs.

She opened the door of the morning-room and ushered him inside. "This delightful gentleman was wrongly told that you weren't at home," said Felicity blithely. She shut

64

the door on Mr. Callaghan and on the Tribbles' outraged faces and went on up to her room, whistling merrily.

"You shouldn't ought to have done that," growled Wanstead, following her. "You did that out of spite and I hopes Miss Amy makes you pay for it."

Felicity remembered the cobra and felt a momentary stab of fear. She was sure the thing had been stuffed and had correctly assumed that it had been a present from that elderly nabob, Mr. Haddon. But her fright on that terrible evening had been so great, she still had nightmares about it. Then she shrugged. She would get the better of Amy yet and, in fact, was almost ready to make her escape.

Felicity, for all her odd upbringing, was very much a young lady of this second decade of the nineteenth century. Amy was, on the contrary, very much of the eighteenth, where ladies had been as broad-spoken as men, and even the highest aristocratic dames in society were as tough as old boots. Felicity was used to despising her own sex as being weak and feeble-minded and had not yet realized quite how tough the Tribble sisters could be. Nor did she realize that it was perhaps Effy she had more to fear, and that delicate and fragile Effy could make a nastier enemy than her mannish sister any day.

Felicity had been working on a susceptible chambermaid, having got the idea from the romance she had been reading. The chambermaid, Charlotte, was a young Cockney girl, easily flattered by Lady Felicity's confidences. She listened wide-eyed as Felicity fed her stories of persecution at the hands of the Tribbles and how they meant to force her to marry the wicked Lord Ravenswood. Finding that Charlotte could read, Felicity lent her the romance, which was all that was needed to make sure that the gullible girl believed every word. Since the apple-pie-bed episode, Felicity was never allowed to leave the house unchaperoned.

Downstairs in the morning-room, the atmosphere was arctic.

"Sit down, Mr. Callaghan, and state your business," said Amy.

"You have stolen my inheritance," said Mr. Callaghan.

"Good heavens," exclaimed Effy. "The man is quite mad. It was *you* who stole *our* inheritance, Mr. Callaghan."

"Mrs. Cutworth left nothing but debts and more debts," said Mr. Callaghan. "By the time I sold the house and contents, there was nothing left for me. I know now why the poor dear lady died penniless. You wicked pair had been cajoling vast sums out of her."

"Fiddle," said Effy. "We believed her to be rich as well."

"Mrs. Cutworth told me you had not a penny," said Mr. Callaghan. "She used to laugh about it. I once came and studied your house. Not a servant in sight. I asked in society. It was well known neither of you had a feather to fly with. But now you live in magnificence and there can only be one answer. I saw that maid of Mrs. Cutworth enter here earlier. Ho! Yes! I have been watching your comings and goings. With her help, you stole Mrs. Cutworth's jewels and tormented the poor woman on her deathbed into giving you her money."

"Have you finished?" said Amy, getting to her feet.

Mr. Callaghan rose as well.

"I shall prove you are thieves and liars if it takes me,to my dying day," he said passionately.

Felicity was descending the stairs when the door of the morning-room opened. Amy came out holding Mr. Callaghan by the seat of his pants and the scruff of his neck. As Felicity watched, Amy frog-marched him down the steps, the butler leaped to open the street door, and Amy threw the beau down the steps, where he rolled over the pavement and into the road.

Amy dusted her hands and then turned to the butler. The butler was explaining something. Amy turned and looked up to where Felicity was standing. Felicity backed up the stairs to her room. How would Amy retaliate?

Felicity woke with a start that night, immediately aware there was someone in her bedroom. Amy, was her first thought. "Who is there?" she cried sharply.

A scared whisper answered her. "Charlotte."

Felicity lit the bed candle from the rushlight. Charlotte, the chambermaid, was standing there, holding something behind her back.

"What are you doing?" demanded Felicity. "And what are you hiding?"

Charlotte began to sob. She brought her hand out from behind her back and held it out. She was clutching several pairs of garters.

"What are you doing with my garters?" asked Felicity.

"I was taking them away," said Charlotte. "Oh, my lady, I was feared you would do yourself a mischief."

Felicity felt a sharp pang of conscience. A maid in one of the neighbouring houses had, only the other day, hanged herself in her garters, a very common form of suicide. Felicity felt she should not have played on the innocent chambermaid's sympathies with her lies of persecution.

Then she hardened her heart. The Tribbles must be punished and she had a simply marvellous plan and Charlotte was important to that plan.

"Do not cry, Charlotte," she said softly. "I am going to escape and you are to help me."

"How, my lady?" asked Charlotte, mopping her eyes with a corner of her apron.

"I used to wear men's clothes in the country," said

67

Felicity, "but I was not allowed to bring such apparel to Town. I shall furnish you with money and bit by bit you must buy me an outfit suitable for a young man about Town. You must go to the very best of the second-hand clothes shops, for I do not want to wear dirty and soiled things."

"Oh, my lady, what if I am caught? Jobs are hard to find."

"I shall look after you. It is your duty to help me, Charlotte. I cannot trust any of the other servants, as they have probably been with the Tribbles for a long time."

Charlotte hesitated. She knew very well that she and the other servants belonged to the Marquess of Ravenswood. But Mr. Humphrey, the butler, had made her swear on the Bible along with the others never to reveal this secret.

"I shall help you in any way I can, my lady," said Charlotte.

"Good," said Felicity, lying back. "Leave my garters and go."

Felicity lay awake for some time after the maid had gone, thinking with pleasure of the Tribbles' shame and consternation when they found her gone. "Mother will never send me back," said Felicity to the candlestick. "Never. I shall make sure of that. She will never trust me to the Tribbles again. But they seem to be coming to their senses. I was so sure Amy would think up some punishment to revenge herself on me."

She did not know she was being discussed at that very moment. Amy was lying in bed, crying, while Effy held her hand.

"I feel I cannot go on any longer," said Amy, taking out a handkerchief the size of a bed sheet and blowing her nose with a great trumpeting sound.

Effy felt a hardening inside her as she looked at her

weeping sister. Felicity must be schooled, and she, Effy, would do it. She patted Amy's hand. "Do nit wirry, eh will d' sumthin abitit."

"For heaven's sake!" snapped Amy, rallying. "Take off that chin-strap. I cannot hear a word you are saying."

Effy unfastened the chin-strap and said clearly, "Do not worry, I will do something about it. I am surprised you are so overcome."

"It was such a piece of petty spite," said Amy. "She knew Callaghan had been told we were not at home."

"Yes, and subjected us both to a most distressing scene," said Effy. "Lady Felicity shall be punished, never fear. It serves him right after all his plotting to end up with nothing. It serves him . . ." Effy began to giggle. "Oh, Amy," she said. "He was *so* very angry."

Amy looked at her in surprise and then she began to laugh as well. She laughed so hard that she quite forgot to ask Effy how she planned to punish Felicity.

A surprised Felicity was awakened two mornings later at seven o'clock and ordered to present herself in the drawing-room in half an hour.

Too sleepy to protest, she allowed Wanstead to dress her and made her way downstairs.

Effy was sitting in the drawing-room with a middle-aged gentleman in a clerical collar.

"Sit down, Lady Felicity," said Effy. "This is the Reverend Tobias Jiggs, a very famous evangelical preacher. Mr. Jiggs, Lady Felicity Vane. You may begin."

To Felicity's horror, Mr. Jiggs got to his feet and began to roar out a sermon on obedience and decorum and the role of a young woman in society. He had very thick lips and dribbled and spat as he spoke. The room was very cold. Effy had not ordered the fire to be lit, considering a cold drawing-room as a sort of mortification that was good for the soul.

Shivering in thin muslin and bludgeoned by words, Felicity sat, wondering when this torture would end. The sermon went on all morning.

When it was over, she heard Effy say, "Delightful, Mr. Jiggs. We shall expect you at the same time tomorrow. As you know, we planned to take Lady Felicity to a concert at the Argyle Rooms tonight, but we have cancelled the outing on your advice."

Felicity escaped to her room, shaking with rage. Now more than ever was she determined to escape.

Chapter 5

. . . they've made him a Dandy;
A thing, you know, whiskered, great-coated,
and laced,
Like an hour-glass, exceedingly small in the
waist,
Quite a new sort of creatures, unknown yet to
scholars,
With heads so immovably stuck in shirt collars,
That seats like our music-stools soon must be
found them,
To twirl, when the creatures wish to look round
them.
Thomas Moore, The Fudge Family in Paris

I T WAS THAT INDIAN cobra which gave Felicity a quiet escape.

Humphrey, the butler, came upon a stranger in the hall. The stranger appeared to be a slim man with most of his face shielded by ginger whiskers.

"Who are you, sir?" demanded Humphrey suspiciously. "I heard no knock."

Behind those whiskers, firmly secured with gum arabic, Felicity quailed. The butler's gooseberry eyes were hard and suspicious.

"I am Lady Felicity's brother," said Felicity haughtily.

Humphrey spent his spare time studying the family trees of the aristocracy. He backed towards the bell-rope, which hung in a corner of the hall. "Lady Felicity does not possess a brother," he said.

Before Felicity could summon up the courage to try to push her way past him to the door, there was an eldritch screech and cries for help from the drawing-room up-stairs.

Humphrey leaped for the stairs with amazing agility in one so fat and pompous. Felicity opened the door and let herself out and walked as quickly as she could down to the corner and turned into Oxford Street.

Upstairs in the drawing-room, all was chaos.

Amy had hugged Mr. Haddon's present to herself. She had sent him a warm letter of thanks but had not told Effy, for Effy, she felt sure, would have sneered and said that no one ever sent *her* such odd presents. Gentlemen had always sent her flowers or poems. So Amy had put the cobra in a cupboard under the glass-fronted book-shelves in the drawing-room.

Effy had been poking about, looking for a spare vase. She had opened the cupboard, found herself faced with the stuffed cobra, and had started to scream the place down. Everyone came running and the air was full of a babble of screams and cries. A footman, taking one horri-fied look at the thing in the cupboard, had fled to return with a blunderbuss. He fired at the cobra, but missed the cupboard completely and peppered a portrait of the third Marchioness of Ravenswood with a volley of nails.

By the time Effy was calm enough to hear Amy's expla-nation, the Marquess of Ravenswood had arrived, unheralded, on the scene, having decided to make one of his impromptu visits to London.

He found himself hard put not to laugh as Amy proudly stood guard over the horrible stuffed snake and said defiantly it was *her* present and no one was to touch it.

Meanwhile, wild rumours were circulating in the servants' hall, and the shaking chambermaid, Charlotte, was convinced someone was dead.

Her poor head, stuffed by Felicity with romantic tales, led her to believe that Felicity had taken her own life. She rushed up to the drawing-room and flung herself weeping on the middle of the carpet and begged for mercy.

There were more screams and cries for explanation. Charlotte cried out that she had known they would drive Lady Felicity to her death with their persecution and they could kill her as well.

Amy took charge, pushing the shocked and enraged butler away. She smoothed the chambermaid's hair and raised her up and asked her gently and patiently to begin at the beginning and tell them what Felicity had said, assuring the girl over and over again that Lady Felicity was well.

In a halting voice, Charlotte told her story, of how Felicity planned to escape, and of how she had bought her men's clothes.

"Get Lady Felicity here immediately," ordered the marquess.

They all waited. Then Humphrey returned to say Lady Felicity had gone.

"You may pack your bits and pieces and leave immediately," said the butler to Charlotte.

"No," said Amy. "The girl stays. Felicity's played a wicked trick on the silly child. Now, where's she gone?"

Humphrey surveyed them, a look of dismay on his

face. "My lord," he said, turning to the marquess. "Just before I heard Miss Effy scream, there was a fellow in the hall. He said he was Lady Felicity's brother. I said Lady Felicity did not have a brother and was about to ring for help when all the fuss started and I ran upstairs."

"It must have been that wretched girl in disguise," said the marquess. "What did she look like?"

"But it could not be she," said Humphrey. "My lord, this person had whiskers."

"Have you never heard of false whiskers, man?" demanded the marquess. "There is even a shop which supplies them to the cavalry. What colour were they? What was she wearing?"

"It is dark in the hall, my lord," said Humphrey, "but a ray of sunlight shone on the whiskers and they appeared to be very red. He—she—was wearing a greatcoat with a nipped-in waist, a bottle-green colour I think, a very high collar, and top boots. The hat was an ordinary beaver with a curly brim."

"Get every man in this household out to search for her," commanded the marquess. He turned to the Tribbles. "Do not look so distressed, ladies. I shall go myself and try to bring her back."

Felicity strolled along in the direction of the City, where she hoped to find a stage-coach to take her to Sussex. Spring had come to London. A warm wind was gusting and blowing down the streets, setting the striped awnings at the windows of the houses flapping and the buff-coloured blinds over the shops cracking and swelling, so that at times it appeared as if the Town were one great sailing-ship under full canvas, straining to leave port.

Whistling as she walked and enjoying her new freedom

and the pleasure of her splendid disguise, Felicity had already forgotten about the Tribbles. That chapter of her life was over. Sussex and home and riding across the Downs on just such a splendid day as this lay ahead.

She went into a coffee-house in Holborn and ordered a meat pie and a bottle of wine. She drank the whole bottle and felt tipsy and ridiculously happy as she set out again.

It was only when she made her way down to the Strand, now determined to have a stroll about London before leaving, that she realized that all mayhem could be breaking loose in one part of the Town while the other parts remained unaware of it.

A mob was rampaging down the Strand, smashing into any shops which had been foolish enough to remain open. Sobered with fright, she retreated back to Holborn and so on to Snow Hill and the City of London, the original walled London where all the commerce of the nation now took place.

She had just entered Candlewick Ward, when a constable seized her and demanded her name.

"Felix Vane," said Felicity in as gruff a voice as she could manage.

"Address?"

"Bread Lane," said Felicity, remembering a City address from an article in the newspapers.

"Householder?"

"Yes," said Felicity, not wanting to have to tell more lies than necessary. For if she said she was not a householder, then that would lead to more and more questions.

"Good, follow me. You will be sworn in as a special constable."

"What for?" said Felicity, her knees beginning to tremble.

"What for?" echoed the constable contemptuously. "Why, to put down them murdering rioters."

And so it was that Lady Felicity Vane, with fixed bayonet and drawn sword, found herself marching over Westminster Bridge surrounded by men equally armed to put down the rioters. She wanted to know why the mob were rioting, she desperately did not want to have to shoot anyone or to have to plunge that wicked-looking bayonet into someone's breast, but was frightened to speak lest her voice should give away her sex.

The sun beat down, her head throbbed in time to the beating of the drums, and she wondered whether she would come out of the whole business alive.

But as it turned out, she was to be more at risk from her fellows than from the rioters. The mob had massed in St. George's Fields. But no sooner did they hear the drums and see the sun glinting on the bayonets of the forces of law and order than they quickly dispersed. Not a shot was fired. Felicity sighed with relief. Now all she had to do was march quietly back and return her weapons to the City armoury and find that stage-coach.

But once she had got rid of her weapons, she was quickly surrounded by her fellow warriors, who declared their intention of getting as drunk as possible and then raising the skirts of every tart to be found within the walls of the City. They went on to describe in graphic detail what they would do to said tarts, and Felicity choked and tried not to vomit in front of them.

"If you will forgive me," she said, finding her voice, but trying to keep it on as low a register as possible, "I must be on my way."

"Stuff," said the leader of her persecutors. "You'll have a few bumpers first." They were out in the street now and he had taken her arm in a strong grasp.

"Oho, nephew," said a languid voice. "I wondered why you were late for dinner."

Felicity looked up into the mocking eyes of the Marquess of Ravenswood. Her companions fell back before the magnificence of the marquess's dress. White as paper behind her whiskers, Felicity fell into step beside the marquess. They walked in silence until the marquess stopped outside a coffee-house. "I think we should have some conversation before I return you home," he said.

He led the way into the coffee-house and found them a table in the corner. He ordered coffee and biscuits.

"How did you find me?" asked Felicity sulkily.

"If you saw those ridiculous whiskers of yours in the clear light of day, you would know they are as red as a Runner's waistcoat. There were many people on your road to the City who remembered an odd-looking fellow with scarlet whiskers. I caught up with you just as you were being pressed into service. I decided to follow you, for tempers were running high at that point and I did not want to risk ruining your reputation by unmasking you. I waited until you had returned to the armoury and then picked my moment."

"I was going home to Sussex," said Felicity, hanging her head.

"And you were making sure to do it in such a way as to cause the most distress and trouble," he said severely. "That chambermaid you gulled with that farrago of lies. Did you never think of her? She thought you had been killed and was prepared to follow you to the grave. She nearly lost her job, which in these days would have been tantamount to killing her. There is no future for a chambermaid turned off without a reference."

"I did not think she would have told anyone anything

about being party to my escape," said Felicity, enraged with guilt.

"You did not think of anyone other than yourself, and you never have," said the marquess. "You are a colossal bore. Unwomanly women always are. You will go back to the Tribbles and you will behave. Do I make myself clear?"

"You have no right to interfere in my life," said Felicity.

"I do not want to have anything to do with you," snapped the marquess. "But I do not like to see the Tribbles tormented and teased by a spoilt brat like you. You have neither looks nor charm nor wit. Try to do as they say and keep your mouth shut and perhaps some poor fool will marry you for your dowry, for you have nothing to offer a man other than money."

Felicity gasped with shock and rage. "I'll show you," she said, between her teeth. "Just you wait! I shall drive some man mad with passion."

The marquess leaned back in his chair and began to laugh. Finally he said, "If you could only see how you look, sitting there in that horse-collar with those ghastly whiskers and vowing to drive some man mad with passion." He was so amused he did not realize Felicity had begun to cry. Salt tears dribbled down among her whiskers. She took a mouthful of coffee and managed to control herself.

Now she hated the marquess more than the Tribbles, more than anyone in the whole wide world.

Outside, the marquess hailed a hack and directed it to Holles Street.

He leaned his head back and thought of Miss Betty Andrews. *She* would never dream of masquerading as a man. She was soft and curvaceous and beautiful, and he liked the pretty confiding way she had of shyly putting a dimpled hand on his arm and smiling up at him. She would never cause him a day's upset or distress. He knew she would be in London for the Season, but, all in that moment, he decided to propose to her before she left Sussex.

Lady Felicity was in bed, and the marquess had just finished telling the Tribbles of Felicity's adventures over a late supper. Effy clucked with shock and distress, but Amy remained silent. Amy thought it was terribly brave of Felicity to go through with allowing herself to be armed and pressed into service as a special constable. Amy also thought it must be wonderful to wear whiskers and stride free down the streets.

"So, ladies," said the marquess, "to turn to pleasanter subjects: Will you dance at my wedding?"

Hope shone in Amy's eyes. "Oh, you monster," she said, "to plague us with your disgust of poor Felicity. Of course we will dance at your wedding. She is young and headstrong, but I knew all along you, above all, would be clever enough to see the gold there."

"I fear Lord Ravenswood does not mean Felicity," said Effy quietly.

"No, of course not," said the marquess. "I mean to wed Miss Betty Andrews."

"Never heard of her," said Amy in a flat voice.

"All London will soon know of her when she takes the Town by storm this coming Season," said the marquess. "She is divinely fair."

"Blondes ain't fashionable," said Amy, leaning forward earnestly, oblivious of the fact that her left elbow was resting in the butter dish. "You can't tell with blondes. Hardly ever natural. Look at Sally Jersey."

"Everything about Miss Andrews is natural," said the marquess with a reminiscent smile.

"And that," as Amy said later to Effy, "is that. I could wring Felicity's neck. How shall we punish her?"

Effy sighed. "I think this time, Amy, we will try kindness, and see if that doesn't shame her into good behaviour. She had quite a terrible experience, you know. Mayhap it has sobered her."

And, in the days that followed, Felicity certainly appeared a changed person. She had had a bad shock and went about quietly and carefully, like someone recovering from an accident.

Charlotte, the chambermaid, had been sent to the marquess's country home, not in disgrace, but to keep her away from Felicity's evil influence. The other servants, even Felicity's maid, Wanstead, kept a wary eye on her but refused to be lured into any conversation. So Felicity settled down and learned to dance the new dances, the quadrille and the waltz, to perfection, play the pianoforte competently, and paint water-colours which gradually began to look like the scenes they were supposed to represent. Her tutors claimed themselves satisfied, particularly the music teacher, who refused to accept that Felicity had already known how to play the piano well and claimed credit for her prowess. The dancing master said she had acquired a certain grace and no longer whooped her way through Scottish reels and country dances like a hoyden.

What the Tribbles themselves were at pains to teach Felicity were courtesy and social manners tempered with kindness. Amy was often graceless and foul-mouthed; Effy, silly; but both had a horror of hurting people by an ill-thought word or clumsy gesture. It was Effy who decided that Felicity must be taught the proper art of flirting. Effy acted as tutor, and Amy, dressed in breeches and bottle-green coat, acted the part of the man. Felicity was trained how to look coyly down when receiving a pretty compliment, how to slap with her fan when receiving a saucy one, and how to shudder and look distressed should the gentleman prove to be overbold in his attentions. Mr. Haddon, coming upon them during one of these sessions, gallantly offered to play the courtier's part; but for some reason Felicity could not understand, Effy grew distressed, and Amy, bad-tempered and sulky. Effy at last told Mr. Haddon it was not seemly that a real gentleman should take part in their learning charades and Amy once more resumed her role.

The Tribbles still only took Felicity to sedate occasions, to lectures or concerts. They did not want Felicity led astray by some unsuitable man before the Season began. And then, a few weeks before the opening ball at Almack's Assembly Rooms in King Street, Lord Bremmer came to call.

The sisters saw no reason to show him the door. He was rich and titled and unattached. Felicity could hardly be expected to do better. Mr. Haddon had told the sisters they had been flying too high when they expected a paragon like Ravenswood even to look at Felicity.

For her part, Felicity was glad to see Lord Bremmer. He was as young as she, and it was flattering to see the love and devotion in his eyes. Ravenswood's insults still burnt like acid in Felicity's breast.

She no longer lay awake at nights making up plots and plans to trounce the Tribbles. But the day after Lord Bremmer's reappearance, the morning papers carried the announcement of the Marquess of Ravenswood's engagement to Miss Betty Andrews. The Tribble sisters had not seen any reason to warn Felicity of the approaching engagement.

Felicity hated the marquess more than ever. He would parade that horrible, clinging idiot, Betty Andrews, in front of her. He would laugh and sneer. The only way she could strike back at him was to hurt the Tribbles.

She was still young enough to consider anyone over the age of twenty-five as being practically devoid of feeling. As far as Felicity was concerned, the Tribble sisters were in comfortable circumstances. They did not need her and would soon find another to replace her.

Lord Bremmer was to be allowed to take her out driving that day. Felicity began again to plot and plan.

She had very little time to force their brief acquaintanceship on to a more intimate footing, but no sooner had they driven off than Lord Bremmer himself gave her the opportunity.

"You must wonder, Lady Felicity," he said, as he turned his phaeton in at the gates of Hyde Park, "why it was I did not follow you to London."

"Yes, I did," said Felicity, giving him a melting smile.

"Well, the awkward fact was," he said, "that a marriage had been more or less arranged for me by my parents. I had to extricate myself from that, don't you see?"

"Oh, yes," breathed Felicity while she fought with her conscience. She hoped desperately that Lord Bremmer's intended had not been too hurt by his rejection of her.

"But the thing that puzzles me," said Lord Bremmer, "is that if Ravenswood wants you for himself, then why did he up and propose to someone else?"

Felicity was ready for that one. "I spurned his advances," she said in a trembling voice. "But he has vowed to get his revenge."

"Gad! How?"

"He has sworn I shall never marry anyone, and to that end, he has persuaded the Tribble sisters to turn anyone from the doors who might wish me as a wife."

"But they gave me a great welcome."

Felicity heaved a melancholy sigh. "I heard them laughing about it afterwards," she said. "Miss Amy said, 'Bremmer is too young to be of danger.' "

Lord Bremmer's face darkened with anger.

"But after tomorrow, I shall not be allowed to see you again," said Felicity, with a break in her voice. "For Ravenswood comes to Town."

"Damme," said Lord Bremmer. "Such cruel persecution is beyond all bounds. I've a good mind to elope with you."

He reined in his horses and looked at her. Felicity's eyes were shining with hero worship.

"Oh, *thank you,*" she said.

"Eh, what?" asked Lord Bremmer, looking at her stupidly.

"Thank you for rescuing me," said Felicity. "My hero!"

"Oh, Gad, what, I say . . . urgh . . ."

"And it can all be so simple. For there is to be a review in Hyde Park at eleven in the morning. And you shall take me to that and then we can change to your travelling carriage and go to Gretna."

"Urm . . . !"

"How brave and clever you are." And Felicity went on praising him and smiling at him and telling him how wonderful he was until the bewildered young man would gladly have taken her to Greenland that very moment had she asked him.

"And I shall put clothes in a paper parcel and say we are dropping them off at St. George's for the poor," said Felicity, "for I could never manage to carry a trunk out of the house."

"No, indeed," said Lord Bremmer, allowing himself to be swept along.

Felicity was resting in her room later that day when Amy came in.

"Ravenswood's coming here this evening," she said abruptly, "with Miss Andrews and her mother. Wear something really good for dinner."

"Is Lord Ravenswood to stay here again?" asked Felicity.

"Yes."

"Why? He has a Town house."

"Er . . . it's being redecorated. Goodness, I'm tired," groaned Amy. "I had hoped for a quiet evening. I do not think I shall enjoy the company of this Miss Andrews. She sounds just the sort of female to make me feel awkward."

"Lord Ravenswood is very close to you, is he not?" asked Felicity.

"What? Oh, yes. Devilishly fond of me and Effy, he is. Anyway, wear one of the new gowns Mamselle made for you, there's a good child."

"Very well, Miss Amy," said Felicity meekly.

Amy eyed her suspiciously.

"I should be glad you are behaving so well these days, but such good behaviour from such as you makes me feel nervous. Not plotting anything, are you?"

"No," said Felicity with a limpid look. "I am become all that is respectable, and the highly respectable Lord Bremmer is to take me to the review in Hyde Park tomorrow."

Amy's face cleared. "He's a pleasant chap and comes from a good family. I had best go and try to make myself as near a fashion-plate as I can. Thank goodness, Mr. Haddon is to be there as well."

As she sat in the drawing-room before dinner, Amy began to fidget nervously. What could be keeping Felicity? Effy was talking to Mr. Haddon, the marquess was standing by the fireplace chatting to Miss Andrews,

84

which left Amy with the task of talking to Mrs. Andrews. Amy could not help wondering whether the marquess ever considered that his beloved might turn out in later years to look like her mother. Mrs. Andrews had been a great beauty in her youth, but discontent had scored lines down either side of her mouth, and an excess of the use of blanc had pitted her skin. She had a high, drawling, affected voice.

Amy was just about to ring the bell and ask a servant to go and fetch Felicity when the door opened and that young lady walked in.

Amy's eyes misted with pride.

The French dressmaker had already lived up to and beyond Amy's expectations. The gown Felicity was wearing was a simple sprigged muslin. But it was one of the finest examples of Yvette's art. The neckline was cleverly cut so that Felicity was allowed to bare the genteel maximum of seductive bosom and still look like a lady. The deep flounces at the hem fluttered as she moved, as did the thin material of her gown, emphasizing the hint of a shapely leg and the young swell of a firm buttock. Her hair was dressed in one of the latest Roman styles and pomaded to a high shine.

Miss Andrews looked at Felicity and then sharply upwards at the marquess. He was watching Felicity with a brooding, hooded look.

Effy made the introductions.

"La," cried Miss Andrews, waving her fan. "I could not for a moment imagine you wearing red whiskers, Lady Felicity."

Felicity gave a half-smile. The Tribble sisters threw reproachful glances at the marquess, who coloured slightly. He had told Miss Andrews of his adventures with Felicity but had not dreamt for a minute she would repeat them to anyone or betray in public that she knew anything at all. But worse was to come. For it soon transpired that Betty Andrews had told her mother all about Felicity. Like her daughter, Mrs. Andrews was irritated by Felicity's appearance. The marquess living under the same roof as the noisy masculine type of female she had expected Lady Felicity to prove to be was one thing; the marquess sharing a home with a graceful enchantress was another.

"Yes, I confess I was monstrous shocked to hear of your escapade," drawled Mrs. Andrews. "Gels were whipped for such behaviour in my day."

The marquess found himself hoping Felicity would say something pert or rude so that he might not feel so awful about the behaviour of his future mother-in-law, but she merely raised her eyebrows slightly and went to sit beside Mr. Haddon.

The rest of the evening was a nightmare for the marquess. It became all too plain that his fiancée was jealous of Lady Felicity, and the more jealous she became, the more charmingly Felicity behaved. After dinner, Felicity entertained the small company by playing the piano. Mr. Haddon clapped enthusiastically and then demanded to see Felicity's latest water-colours, telling Mrs. Andrews proudly that Felicity had a professional touch.

The marquess watched Felicity with a brooding gaze. He found himself wondering if she had become beautiful, enchanting, and accomplished merely to spite him.

When at last Mrs. Andrews rose to her feet and said they must leave, the remaining company sighed with relief.

Amy came back into the drawing-room after seeing the Andrewses off.

Felicity was putting away her sheets of music. Amy slapped her on the back. "You Trojan, Felicity," she said.

86

"If you weren't the most enchanting piece of goods I've seen in years."

Felicity smiled and blushed, but something flashed in the depths of her eyes.

Amy thought uneasily that the quick flash had been one of guilt and wondered why.

Chapter 6

There is a tide in the affairs of women,
Which, taken at the flood, leads—God knows
where

Lord Byron, Don Juan

DESCENDING THE STAIRS THE following morning, the Marquess of Ravenswood paused. Felicity was leaving to go to the review in Hyde Park with Lord Bremmer. Amy and Effy were seeing them off. Felicity, the marquess noticed, was clutching a huge parcel.

"What on earth is in that parcel?" he called.

The little group turned to face him. Amy and Effy were smiling, Lord Bremmer scowling, and Felicity looking defiant.

"Lady Felicity is going to drop off a parcel of her old clothes at St. George's," said Effy.

"And you on your way to see the review!" said the

marquess, descending the stairs. "I shall be passing St. George's myself this morning. Allow me to deliver the parcel for you."

"That will not be necessary," said Felicity. Lord Bremmer had turned a muddy colour. "Let us go," added Felicity impatiently. The marquess watched them with narrowed eyes as they collided in the doorway in their haste to escape.

"Why do you look so angry?" asked Amy. "Bremmer is all that is suitable, although I confess I would have thought a man slightly older than Felicity would be more the thing."

"I think she's up to mischief," said the marquess. He turned to the hovering butler. "Fetch that female here—the French dressmaker."

"What do you want to see Yvette for?" asked Amy. "Does Miss Andrews wish her services? For she can't have 'em, you know. Yvette is *my* find. And she's busy now, making clothes for me and Effy."

"You'll see" was all the marquess would say.

Yvette appeared behind the butler. She was a young Frenchwoman in her twenties, with black eyes, a sallow skin, neatly dressed brown hair, and a trim figure.

"Follow me, Yvette," said the marquess.

"Shall we go and see what he is up to?" asked Effy as the marquess strode up the stairs, with the dressmaker scurrying after him.

"No," said Amy. "You never can tell with gentlemen. Their moods are most odd. He is probably going to get her to make Miss Andrews' wedding gown or something like that and does not want to offend us."

The marquess led the way into Felicity's bedchamber. It looked as if a bomb had hit it. Yvette clucked in dismay. Clothes were lying everywhere, where they had been dragged from drawers and closets.

"Now, Yvette," said the marquess. "You should know the contents of Lady Felicity's wardrobe by now. Tell me which clothes are missing."

The maid quickly began to search the room. "That new gold silk pelisse with the swansdown trimming is missing," she said half to herself, as she looked, "and the pink muslin with the five flounces, and the green carriage dress with the frogs, and—"

"Enough! I gather these were not old."

"Oh no, my lord. They were my best creations and Lady Felicity seemed to like them."

"That will be all," said the marquess.

He hurried down to the drawing-room and confronted the sisters. "It is my considered opinion," he said, "that Lady Felicity has eloped with Bremmer. The clothes in that parcel were her best."

Effy let out a faint scream, but Amy said robustly, "Why would she do that?"

"To have her revenge," said the marquess. "To disgrace us all. It is of no use my going to the review. I am sure they will not be there. They are probably on the road north. Do not worry. I shall punch Bremmer's head and bring her back. She can have Bremmer if she wants, but in church and properly. The devil! I was to take Miss Andrews driving. Send a footman with my apologies."

After he had left, the sisters sat looking stricken. "Can he be mistaken?" said Effy at last. "Lady Felicity must know what this means. Not only will Lady Baronsheath be furious, but no one in society will ever want our services. Oh, Amy. Back to the days of cold rooms and stewed scrag-end of mutton."

"I hope she breaks her neck," said Amy savagely. "Of all the cruel and spiteful little minxes . . . Oh, why did we have to advertise for difficult girls. I didn't like that Miss

Andrews, but now she seems like all that is good and worthy in comparison to Felicity."

All went well with the eloping couple. It was another fine spring day. Great fleecy clouds sailed overhead as they sat up on the box of Lord Bremmer's travelling carriage. Lord Bremmer had no regrets. Every time he turned to look at Felicity she gave him a soft, glowing smile. He felt ten feet tall. He was sure his parents' fury would be short-lived when they learned he had had the good sense to elope with a titled heiress.

Confident that no one would be looking for them for some time, as the review was expected to last for over two hours, they broke their journey at a posting house in Barnet. They had been sitting amicably side by side in the coffee-room, drinking coffee and eating cake, when Felicity excused herself.

"Where are you going?" asked Lord Bremmer.

"To the Jericho," said Felicity calmly.

Lord Bremmer blushed painfully. He felt it was very unwomanly of Felicity to be so graphic. She should have said she was retiring to straighten her gown or something like that.

When Felicity had left, he picked up an old copy of *The Morning Post* and idly studied the advertisements on the front.

The Tribbles' advertisement seemed to leap out of the page at him. Felicity had confided in him that her misguided mother had answered an advertisement in *The Morning Post*. But surely it could not be this one—"If you have a Wild, Unruly, or Undisciplined Daughter . . ."

He put the paper down and shook his head as if to clear it. This could not be the one. It must have been some other advertisement.

He sipped his cooling coffee and waited, and waited. At last, fearing something might have happened to Felicity, he sent a maid to the privy in the inn garden to see if she was still there. But before the maid returned, Felicity erupted into the coffee-room, her eyes shining.

"Such luck," she cried. "I have bespoke a couple of hunters for us."

"Gad! Hunters? Why?"

"The hunt, man. The hunt. They are already off and running."

"You cannot mean to join a hunt in the middle of an elopement."

Felicity stamped her foot. "No one will be after us for hours. It is a perfectly splendid day and the scent is high. Here! Give me that parcel. I must change."

She seized her brown paper parcel and ran out.

His mouth in a firm line of disapproval, Lord Bremmer went out into the inn courtyard to cancel the order for the hunters. But the landlord had been impressed by Felicity's forceful personality and said he would not do anything until he had the lady's permission.

Felicity appeared dressed in the men's clothes the chambermaid had bought her, but minus the greatcoat and whiskers.

Lord Bremmer closed his eyes at the sight of his beloved in breeches, top boots, and padded coat. She looked like an effete and shoddy Dandy, fallen on hard times.

"Don't fall asleep," laughed Felicity. "Up and away, Bremmer, or we'll lose them."

When Lord Bremmer opened his eyes, it was to see Felicity leaping into the saddle.

"I—I say," he called desperately. "Gad, Lady Felicity. Oh, Gad."

With a turnip grin on his face, the landlord was leading

a hunter forward. "Better get mounted, my lord," he said, "or you'll lose your lady."

The marquess, sure that the couple would not try to break their journey anywhere until nightfall, pressed on through Barnet. The *we-aw, we-aw, we-aw* of a hunting-horn was sounding over the fields to his right. He brought his attention back to the road just in time. A section of the road had fallen in, probably having been cracked and undermined by the winter's frosts. By forcing his team round by the narrow grass verge, he just managed to miss it. He glanced back over his shoulder. Had he not been in such haste to catch Felicity, he would have cut a stave and tied a handkerchief on top of it and fixed it in the hole as a warning to other drivers.

He stopped eventually at a large posting house to change his horses and inquire after the couple. But it had been a quiet day, they said, with hardly any traffic on the road. The marquess was puzzled. He began to wonder whether he had made a mistake, whether the couple had gone to the review after all.

He hesitated before driving on. He sat, holding the reins loosely in his hands. He deliberately banished the image of Felicity as she had looked the previous evening from his brain—that image of a seductive, accomplished, mannered Felicity, which had haunted him ever since. He thought instead of a selfish and spoilt Felicity. And then he remembered the sound of that hunting-horn.

She wouldn't—would she? In the middle of an elopement? But then he doubted if Felicity was in that happy state of mind where the world was well lost for love. It was a gamble. But it was a gamble he decided to take. He swung his team about and headed back towards Barnet.

Night was falling fast, and he studied the landmarks on

either side. He wished now he had marked that hole in the road. But he had noted that, from the direction he was approaching, a weirdly twisted willow stood just at the roadside before it.

He swung round a bend. He saw the willow, outlined against the greenish-purple sky, and then he saw a carriage on its side in the hole. A figure of a man was stooping to cut the traces while another soothed the plunging rearing horses. The slimmer, slighter man led the horses to the side of the road away from the hole.

The marquess reined in his horses, tethered them to a fence and walked forward. The slimmer man suddenly said to the stockier one in a very feminine voice, "Don't start on a jaw-me-dead, Bremmer."

"It's all your stupid fault" came Lord Bremmer's anguished voice. "You *would* take the ribbons. Drive to an inch! Pah!"

"I *can* drive to an inch," howled Felicity furiously, "but John Lade himself would have fallen into that hole in this light."

The marquess darted toward Felicity and clipped her round the waist in a strong grasp from behind. She screamed and twisted and struggled until he punched her on the back of the head and told her to be quiet.

"Now, Bremmer," said the marquess. "You will both get into my carriage and come with me to the nearest posting house till I find out how we can keep your escapade a secret.

He frog-marched Felicity to his open carriage, shouting over his shoulder to Lord Bremmer, "Leave those cursed horses alone. We'll send an ostler for them."

Felicity stopped struggling and sat sullenly beside the marquess. Lord Bremmer climbed in and sat next to her.

"Ravenswood," he cried. "I must explain—"

"Not a word," snapped the marquess, inching his team round both hole and carriage, "until we get to Barnet."

At the inn, he demanded a private parlour and then ushered the guilty couple up the stairs in front of him.

Wine was brought in and the inn servants dismissed before the marquess began in an even voice, "Now, Bremmer, since you could have had her in church, I assume the elopement must have been her idea."

Lord Bremmer made a brave stand although, with a sinking heart, he was already sure everything Felicity had told him was a pack of lies.

Without looking at Felicity, he said, "She told me you wanted her for yourself."

The marquess flicked a contemptuous look at Felicity, who was still dressed in men's clothes. "You must be mad," he said. "My engagement to Miss Andrews has just been announced."

"Lady Felicity said that was because she had spurned your advances," said Lord Bremmer, blushing to the roots of his hair. He looked pleadingly at the marquess's hard face. "Well, she did, and she said although you were to marry Miss Andrews, you had sworn that no other man should have her and had given those sisters instructions to repulse any proposal."

The marquess took a sip of wine and leaned back in his chair. His eyes glittered in the candle-light. "And do you still believe that?" he asked softly.

Lord Bremmer struck the table. "No, by Gad!" he said. "Not a word of it."

"Then," said the marquess in a deceptively mild voice, "perhaps you will be more cautious in future and take what your wife says with a pinch of salt."

"Wife?" Lord Bremmer's mouth fell open in dismay.

"Yes, wife. You shall marry her in church with your parents' blessing after asking both the Tribbles and Lady

Baronsheath formally for their permission to pay your addresses to Lady Felicity. Which is what you should have done in the first place. This sorry episode will be hushed up. Do I make myself clear?"

"I can't marry her!" cried Lord Bremmer. "You must save me from her, Ravenswood."

Felicity, who had been sitting with her head bowed, jerked upright at that and stared at Lord Bremmer with a shocked look on her face.

"Don't be stupid," snapped the marquess. "You were so much in love with the creature that you ran off with her."

"But I did not know what she was like," cried Lord Bremmer. "Oh God, believe me, Ravenswood, she was so winsome, so womanly, and so charming, I—"

"And then unfortunately a fox-hunt threw itself in your path," said the marquess.

"Oh, yes, and she became like a demon," said Lord Bremmer. "We rode and rode and she was shouting and cheering and swearing . . . well, I have never heard such language. But it was a good hunt and we nearly had our fox when she disappeared. I cursed her but separated from the hunt to look for her. I saw her! I saw what she did."

"What?" asked the marquess, glancing curiously at Felicity, whose face had become as red as fire.

"She had a red herring on a string. She must have stolen it from the inn kitchen. She dragged it across the ground and then threw it into a spinney. The hounds picked up the smell of herring and by the time the whole hunt descended on that spinney, she was at the back of them, looking as innocent as anything. Lord! The master's face when his dogs came out of the spinney, quarrelling over that herring! I nearly died of shame."

"I never could stand the kill," said Felicity in a suffocated voice.

"I am glad you have some womanly feelings, however idiotic," said the marquess. "Do you not know the damage foxes do, and you a countrywoman?"

Felicity hung her head.

"Then," said Lord Bremmer, "she drank a bottle of port, and when we set out again, she insisted on taking the reins. I tried to stop her, but she laughed at me and forced me to let her have her way by threatening to get down and walk home."

"You may have the schooling of her when you are married," said the marquess.

"I *won't* marry her," said Lord Bremmer. "Oh, my poor father and mother. Oh, poor Marian, who thought I loved her, and I spurned her and all because of this hoyden. Ravenswood, I beg of you, please do not force me into marriage. I will do anything. I am so ashamed. Please, my lord. Oh, have mercy on me."

Lord Bremmer let out a choked sob and buried his face in his handkerchief.

Felicity was now as white as she had been red a moment before. She had sworn to show the marquess that some man could be mad with passion for her. All she had presented him with was a young man, broken in spirit and near tears at the very idea of having her as his wife.

She felt a hard lump rising in her throat. But she would not cry. The worst was over.

But Felicity was wrong.

"Call on me tomorrow, Bremmer," said the marquess, "and we will discuss this further. Meanwhile, we shall leave you here to attend to the repairs to your carriage. Felicity, finish your wine and come with me."

Felicity would have liked to protest, but she was sure

if she said anything, her control would snap and she would burst into tears.

The tears came at last on the road home. But because of the darkness, the marquess was not aware of them. He talked on and on.

"And did you never think, Lady Felicity," he said, his voice harsh with anger, "of the fate of all those nurses and governesses you are reputed to have had dismissed? Turned off from a noble household? And what of the Tribbles? But it is of no use, and I may as well save my breath. If only the Tribbles or your mother would listen to me! I would tell them to send you to a convent in Belgium and to leave you there until some sense was driven into your head."

Felicity found her voice. "We are not Catholic," she said, "so such talk of a convent is nonsense."

"Talk of any reformation is a waste of time," he snapped. "You are a disgrace to your sex."

To Felicity's relief he fell silent. But her relief was short-lived. For in the ensuing silence, she had time to reflect on the events of the day, to remember the horror and disgust on Lord Bremmer's face. Surely it was all somebody else's fault. But Felicity could not think of any excuse and she ached with shame. All she could pray for was a hasty retreat to her room and the oblivion of sleep.

As they drove through the streets of London in the marquess's open carriage, Felicity was achingly conscious of her appearance. She felt sure everyone looking at her would know she was a girl dressed as a man.

As they drove through the Mayfair streets, they approached a house where a rout was in progress. When holding a rout, it was the tradition to have all the curtains at the windows pulled back. As they came abreast of the mansion, the marquess slowed to allow a lumbering brewer's sledge to cross in front of him. Felicity glanced at the house. A group of people were standing on the steps, waiting for their carriage to be brought round. One of the group was Miss Betty Andrews. She looked full at Felicity and the marquess and her eyes widened. Felicity turned her head away and at that moment the marquess, finding the road clear, flicked the reins and his carriage moved on.

Miss Andrews had been wearing a spangled gown and some sort of sparkling headdress. The marquess had not seen her. Felicity could not help contrasting her own appearance with that of Miss Andrews. She felt she ought to warn the marquess they had been seen, and that she was prepared to swear blind, should Miss Andrews ask, that she was her own mythical brother.

They arrived at Holles Street. There was no hope that the sisters had gone to bed. Lights shone at the windows, and as soon as Felicity climbed down, the door opened and Effy and Amy came out on the step.

Tears blurred Felicity's eyes. She brushed past them and hurtled up the stairs to her room. "Let her go," called the marquess to Amy, who was about to follow Felicity. "Time enough tomorrow to sort things out."

The sisters waited anxiously in the drawing-room while the marquess saw to the stabling of the horses.

"Do you think there is any hope for us?" asked Effy. "He has brought her back, but what of the scandal?"

"We must wait and see," replied Amy, twisting a pleat in her gown with large hands. "We must have been mad to ever hope that Ravenswood would even look kindly on the girl."

The door of the drawing-room opened and the marquess came in. He looked tired and cross. The sisters fussed round him, making him sit in a chair by the fire and plying him with wine and cake.

"Well?" demanded Amy at last. "Are we still in business?"

"Yes, I should think so," said the marquess, leaning his head against the back of the chair and half-closing his eyes. "If today doesn't cure her, then nothing will."

"But the scandal!" cried Effy.

"I do not think there will be any scandal," said the marquess. "Bremmer is terrified he might have to marry her. Listen, I shall tell you all."

The sisters listened in growing amazement to his tale of the elopement, the hunt, and the accident, and Bremmer's sobbing at the very idea of having to marry Felicity.

"But as to what you are to say to her tomorrow, I do not know," ended the marquess.

"I will speak to her," said Effy firmly. "She should be whipped!"

Amy shifted her large feet uneasily. Felicity had admittedly behaved disgracefully, but Amy could not help admiring her. How wonderful it must be to behave really badly, just once.

"And Miss Andrews was here earlier," added Effy, "and asking such questions—where were you, where was Felicity, when were you expected back, and so on, and Mrs. Andrews was worse. Mrs. Andrews thought you should have called in person to give your apologies. Mrs. Andrews wanted to know what you were doing living here. Mrs. Andrews wanted to know a deal of things."

The marquess frowned. "I hope Mrs. Andrews realizes that after I am married, I will not tolerate a mama-in-law being underfoot for most of the day. Lord, I am so tired."

He rose to his feet. Effy studied his broad shoulders, handsome face, long limbs, and let out a little sigh and fluttered her eyelashes at him. He smiled and kissed her hand and she giggled and blushed while Amy scowled.

After Effy had gone to bed, Amy sat at her toilet table,

brushing her hair and wondering what to do about Felicity. At last, she threw down the brush, and pulling a wrapper over her nightgown, she picked up a candle and made her way to Felicity's bedchamber and listened at the door.

She was just about to turn away when she heard a strangled sob coming from inside the room. She pushed open the door and went in.

Felicity was lying face down on the bed, still dressed in her men's clothes.

Amy set her candle down on the table beside the bed and drew up a chair. She took one of Felicity's hands in her own and held it tight.

"There now," said Amy, as if trying to quieten a frightened horse. "Steady, girl."

Felicity turned a blotched and anguished face up from the pillow. "Bremmer was *begging* not to have to marry me," she said.

"Well, you did give him a fright," said Amy reasonably. "Gentlemen are very romantical, you know, and quite put out when you insist on joining a hunt in the middle of an elopement. Something like that once happened to me. You won't tell anyone?"

Felicity dumbly shook her head, surprise drying her eyes. She released her hand from Amy's and twisted round on her back.

"It's a long time ago," sighed Amy. "There was a Mr. Peterson was interested in me and asked Papa permission to take me on a drive to Richmond. It was a fine sunny day, and the further we got from London, the more carefree I felt. I had never been driven very fast, don't you know, and I begged him to go faster and faster, until we were flying along. I had never before felt so happy or so free. I felt drunk. I began to sing at the top of my voice. I was so happy, I did not realize what I was singing. It was a coarse hunting song. I had heard the grooms sing it in the mews and it had amused me and I had learned the words to shock Effy. The long and the short of it was I gave him a disgust of me, and I was very attracted to him, you know. Very. We never got to Richmond. He simply turned his team about and started back to London. I kept pleading with him to tell me what was wrong, although I knew very well what was wrong. He would not say one word, simply drove me straight home and dumped me off and cut me the next time he saw me. Lord, *how* I cried and cried. You see, Felicity, it is all very well for the gentlemen to go roistering or fall down drunk or smash all the windows in Bond Street with their whips; but for us, all must be decorum. But there are marriages, don't you know, where the husband allows his wife quite a lot of freedom, but in order to secure that freedom, one must play the social game first and make sure the gentleman falls very deeply in love. Do you understand?"

Felicity nodded, and then said, "Why aren't you shouting at me?"

"Because of what you did?" Amy shrugged. "Lord, I don't know. Perhaps it is because all your rotten behaviour strikes a sympathetic chord in my heart. But do not go on treating me and Effy like enemies. What were your parents about, not to school you earlier?"

"Papa did not want a girl," said Felicity. "He wanted a son, and I tried to be the sort of son he would have wanted. The wilder I grew, the more he admired me, and I felt I was making up to him for not being a boy."

"But it can be fun being a woman," said Amy, although wondering at the same time what was fun about leading such a restricted life. "When I feel I cannot cope with something, I pretend I am an actress, playing a part. Now, say, why not pretend you are a charming and beautiful woman who can drive men mad, and then practise your wiles on Ravenswood."

Felicity shuddered. "He was worse than Bremmer," she said. "I *hate* him."

"All the more reason to tease him a bit, I would have thought," said Amy. "Oh, I *do* not like that Miss Andrews."

"She saw me," said Felicity miserably.

"The deuce! When?"

Felicity told her.

"We must warn Ravenswood," said Amy. "Let us get you prepared for bed. Where is Wanstead?"

"I told her to go away."

"Well, I am sure you are perfectly well able to put yourself to bed," said Amy, rising and making for the door. "Now, try to behave tomorrow, and I will try to ensure that everything goes on as if nothing had happened."

Feeling comforted, Felicity, after Amy had gone, washed and changed into a clean nightgown. She climbed into bed and fell asleep almost immediately, plunging straight down into a nightmare where all those dismissed governesses and nurses were standing in a circle round her with rocks in their hands, ready to stone her to death.

Chapter 7

Ladies of a certain age,
Means, age uncertain.
—*Lord Byron,* Don Juan

*E*FFY WAS TOLD BY Amy that Felicity had
been well and truly lectured and to
leave matters alone.

Having tossed and turned most of the night, rehearsing
a quite terrible lecture to deliver to Felicity, Effy felt
cheated, and she kept saying she was sure Amy had been
too soft-hearted.

But Felicity's behaviour soon silenced her. Even Amy
would never have dreamt for a moment that Felicity
would apologize for her conduct. But apologize she did,
and in such a low and shaking voice that Effy's heart was
touched and she gave the girl an impulsive hug and told

her to forget all about it and that they would all begin afresh.

"I have noticed," said Effy bracingly, "that you have not yet learned the gentle art of entertaining someone to tea. Sit over there, Felicity, and I shall instruct you."

While Effy had the teapoy, teapot, kettle, and everything else necessary brought in and showed Felicity how to warm the pot, how to leave the tea-leaves to infuse for ten minutes before pouring in the boiling water, and how to hold the cup and saucer, Amy was free to turn her mind to more interesting things, and one of the most interesting things lined up for that day was a visit from Mr. Haddon. She had so many exciting things to tell him and was determined that, this time, Effy should not upstage her.

Mr. Haddon was comfortably seated beside the tea-tray at three o'clock that afternoon. Felicity was quietly playing a haunting little tune on the pianoforte; the marquess was leaning back in a chair, studying her thoughtfully. He felt he should rejoice in her crushed and quiet demeanour, but he could not help wishing irrationally that some of the old Felicity would surface. He wondered what it was she was playing as the sad little tune wound its way round his brain. Effy was chattering away to Mr. Haddon, flirting with her eyes and playing with her fan.

There came a sound of footsteps on the stairs. "That will be Amy," said Effy brightly.

But it was Miss Andrews and her mother who were ushered in.

The marquess thought disloyally that had he taken up residence in his own Town house, then the Andrewses could not have called on him the way they could at the Tribbles' where he was chaperoned. Felicity stopped playing to rise and make her curtsy. She was wearing a gown of white muslin over which she wore a very fine Kashmir shawl in golds and reds which was draped over one shoulder and tied in at the waist. Fine Kashmir shawls were much coveted, and Miss Andrews' beautiful eyes narrowed somewhat as she looked at Felicity.

"Pray go on playing, Lady Felicity," said Effy, after the guests were seated and more cups and cakes had been brought in. Effy was proud of Felicity's prowess.

Felicity gratefully turned back to the piano.

"And where was you yesterday, Ravenswood?" she heard Mrs. Andrews ask.

"I had business to attend to," said the marquess.

"We saw you last night," said Betty Andrews rather shrilly. "We were leaving the Georges' rout and stood on the step when you went past with Lady Felicity and she was dressed in men's clothes!"

Felicity forced herself to continue playing.

"You do Lady Felicity an injustice," said the marquess. "Why on earth would she be dressed in masculine clothes? I was merely bringing that reprobate of a cousin of hers back to Town. The family resemblance is striking, I'll admit."

Betty Andrews smiled, and then flashed her mother an I-told-you-so look. "You must forgive us," said Betty. "But, as you say, the resemblance is striking. I told Mama it was probably some relative of Lady Felicity, but she would have it otherwise."

"That is all very well," said Mrs. Andrews sharply. "But we are all become the subject of lampoons in the print-shops."

The marquess stiffened. Had Bremmer talked? The print-shops were notorious for making artists work all night if necessary in order to lampoon the latest victim as soon as possible.

"What are they saying?" he asked.

"Only that this house is being called Ravenswood's

harem and they are saying that you are Turkish in your tastes and prefer older women."

The marquess laughed, as much with relief as anything else. "If that is all they have to say, let 'em," he said.

"But you must admit it looks very odd," pursued Mrs. Andrews, a high, whining note of complaint entering her voice. "You have a perfectly good Town house which—"

"Which I have let for the Season," said the marquess in a flat voice.

"Do not go on, Mama," said Betty quickly, seeing the look of increasing irritation on the marquess's face. "Lord Ravenswood is quite right. There is no need to make a fuss. The lampoonists will find another subject on the morrow. Let us talk of other things. Shall we see you at the playhouse tomorrow?"

"I am afraid not," replied the marquess. "I attend the opening ball at Almack's."

Betty Andrews turned pink. *She* had not received vouchers to the famous assembly rooms and was still smarting from the snub. The stern patronesses might have unbent and given her the vouchers after her engagement to Ravenswood had not Mrs. Andrews met the Countess Lieven, one of the assembly rooms' sternest despots, in the Park, and harangued that lady, who had obviously delighted in giving Mrs. Andrews a magnificent set-down.

"I am surprised you go, Ravenswood," said Mrs. Andrews, raising her eyebrows. "Why, pray? As you know, my poor Betty has been most disgracefully snubbed."

"I have promised various friends I would be there, that is all," said the marquess repressively, wishing now he had not given in to the sisters' pleas that he should escort Felicity and make sure the girl was well and truly launched on her first Season.

Betty felt miserable. She wished Felicity would stop playing and turn around. There was something which rankled about the expertise of her playing and the elegance of her back presented to the company.

Then the door opened and Amy walked in. Mrs. Andrews tittered. Betty stared, wide-eyed. Effy let out a sort of bleating sound. Felicity stopped playing and turned around.

Amy looked like a guy.

She had bullied Yvette into making her a thin muslin gown with puffed sleeves and flounces, a gown more suitable for a miss in her teens than for a leathery lady of uncertain years. Amy's hair was frizzed and pomaded and decorated with flowers. Her bony arms hung uselessly at her sides, the short gloves revealing elbows like nutmeg graters.

"Whatever have you done to yourself?" cried Effy.

Amy's large feet, clad in pink silk slippers, flapped miserably as she crossed the floor and looked in the glass over the fireplace which had replaced the ruined portrait. Sunlight flooded the room and cruelly showed Amy her own tired and lined face below the ridiculous arrangement of frizzed hair and flowers. What had looked attractive in the candle-lit shadows of her bedchamber now looked grotesque in the full glare of the sunlight. Like many ladies of her age, Amy never prepared her toilet or did her hair with the curtains drawn back, finding the softer light of candles presented a more flattering image of herself to carry through the day. An ugly blush stained her cheeks, and she turned and looked at Mr. Haddon like an old dog who has been whipped.

"You look very fine, Miss Amy," said Felicity in a clear voice, "but it lacks a few touches." She unpinned and untied the huge Kashmir shawl from her own dress and went up to Amy. "Now," said Felicity, "if we unpin all these flowers, *so,* and put the shawl, *so* . . ." She swung the gaily coloured shawl about Amy's shoulders like a cloak and belted it at Amy's waist. The shawl with its glorious, barbaric colours covered most of Amy's gown. The glowing design of the shawl and its heavy gold fringe immediately gave Amy dignity and style. It was a masterstroke.

Mr. Haddon leaped to his feet. "I have brought several fine shawls back with me from India, Miss Amy," he said. "I shall send them round to you and you may have your pick. I declare, I never before saw any lady who could wear the fashion so well."

Amy blushed with pleasure this time. She sat down beside Mr. Haddon and began to talk.

The marquess went over to Betty and then led her over to the window. "You must forgive me," he said. "But I did promise the Tribbles I would help to launch Lady Felicity by taking her to Almack's."

Betty bit her lip. "But it will look most odd," she protested.

"I do not think so. Anyone can see I have no interest in the chit whatsoever."

Betty smiled up at him tremulously and he pressed her hand. She felt reassured, and yet, when Felicity had put that shawl of hers around Amy Tribble's shoulders, there had been a certain warmth in the marquess's eyes when he looked at Felicity that Betty did not like.

Betty wished she could feel more at ease with her fiancé. Her father was a very wealthy squire who had made his fortune by buying a profitable sugar plantation in the West Indies. Her family was of the gentry, not the aristocracy, and very moral and staid in their ways. Securing the marquess had been a great triumph, and that triumph had been better than any love or passion. But for the first time, Betty began to wonder what life would be like after they were married. The marquess was heir to a dukedom. His father was the Duke of Handshire. The idea of being a duchess one day had seemed like a fairy-tale. But now Betty found herself wondering what it would be like to have to control the complicated running of a ducal mansion and a whole army of servants. Her father preferred female servants, strong countrywomen who were not in the least intimidating. In the country, Betty had felt secure in her social position. She knew herself to be the prettiest girl for miles around and a very rich heiress. But in London things were different; her family's wealth ensured her an entrée to most places—but not all. Betty thought it a very unfair world where a hoyden like Felicity could be ensured vouchers to Almack's when she herself could not.

"Lord Bremmer," the butler announced.

Betty noticed the sudden stricken look on Felicity's face and the wild exchange of glances between the sisters and wondered what was wrong.

"What brings you here, Bremmer?" asked the marquess sharply.

"You asked me to call," said Lord Bremmer, colouring up.

"I had forgot," said the marquess. "We had something to discuss, had we not? I had better wait until another time." He introduced his fiancée and Mrs. Andrews.

"But we have met before!" cried Betty.

"I d-do not think so," stammered Lord Bremmer, looking in a bewildered way at the beautiful face turned up to his own. "I could not possibly have forgotten."

"We were both ten years old at the time." Betty laughed. "My parents were staying with relatives near your home and Papa decided to call and make a tour of the house and grounds. I wandered off and climbed an apple tree and became stuck and screamed for help and you got me down."

"By George! So I did," cried Lord Bremmer, remembering that sunny day and the plump little girl who was crying dismally from a branch of the apple tree.

They sat down together and began to talk like old friends.

The marquess crossed to the piano. Felicity's hands faltered on the keys. "What are you playing?" he asked.

"It is a composition of my own."

"Indeed!"

"But I cannot develop it any further."

"It is enchanting as it is. Of course, you could symphony-ize it by putting a lot of chords and flourishes in the left hand. See, like so." He sat down on the long music stool next to her. "Now you play the melody and I shall add the dramatics."

Felicity began to play and he began to elaborate with chords and cadenzas. Felicity began to laugh. "We should perform at the Argyle Rooms," she said. "See, now we cross hands in quite the best manner."

The marquess laughed too and leaned across her. His arm brushed her bosom. His hip on the music stool was pressed against her hip. His fingers suddenly stumbled over the keys.

"I cannot play anymore," he said. He got up and walked away.

Felicity felt suddenly cold. She sat for a few moments with her fingers resting on the keys. Then she raised her hands and began to play a Bach movement with great verve and style.

The Duke and Duchess of Handshire sat discussing their son's forthcoming marriage and agreeing that it was the first time he had ever caused either of them any worry. The marquess had inherited his estates and fortune from an aunt, which had made him independent of his parents. They had mourned their loss of control over him but had been pleasurably surprised when he had continued to lead a fairly quiet, respectable, and hard-working life. They themselves never went to Town, preferring the world to come to them.

Then there had been the letter from the marquess telling them of his engagement, and now there was a letter from old Lord Chumley, informing them that Ravenswood had taken up residence with a couple of old maids and was under the same roof as the wild and beautiful Lady Felicity, which the whole of the world thought most odd.

The duke and duchess found it all most odd as well.

"This Andrews girl is not of our station," said the duchess at last. "A fiancée of his own rank would never have allowed such a state of affairs to exist. He must not marry this girl."

"But we have no power over Charles," said the duke, Charles being Ravenswood's first name.

"If he saw the Andrews girl in these surroundings, he would soon realize he was about to marry beneath him," said the duchess. "It is so long since he has paid us a visit, he has forgotten what the place is like. He forgets what is due to his name. We shall summon them all here— these two old maids, the Tribbles, and Miss Andrews and Lady Felicity. When he sees them all against the background of his family home, he will soon change his mind."

Amy and Effy were to take Felicity to a concert at the Argyle Rooms that evening. But Felicity found herself suffering from a terrible headache. It had been lurking at the back of her temples all day, and when the Andrewses took their leave, it burst on her with full force. Alarmed,

Amy would have decided to stay at home, but Felicity said weakly that all she wanted was to lie down and be left alone. Effy was desperate to go to hear the latest male soprano and Mr. Haddon was to go as well, so Amy was easily persuaded to leave Felicity to be looked after by her maid. As soon as the sisters had left, Felicity dismissed Wanstead, saying that if only she could be left entirely alone and without anyone fussing over her, she was sure the headache would go away.

And as soon as she was alone, that is exactly what happened. The headache miraculously disappeared, leaving Felicity wide-awake and strangely restless. The events of the day before now seemed like some awful dream, the Felicity who had run off with Lord Bremmer a completely different person. She thought about the Marquess of Ravenswood and tried to feel some of the hate she had felt for him the day before, but all she could feel was curiosity about this man who could be such a Tartar one minute and so unexpectedly kind the next.

She rose and dressed, wishing now she had gone to the concert. She wandered out of her room, wondering whether to go down to the drawing-room and pass the evening practising the piano. She hesitated in the corridor outside, listening to the hush of the house. An oil lamp on a stand at the end of the passage shone on the closed door of the marquess's room. What sort of man was he? she wondered. It would be interesting to take a peek inside his room and look about. There could be no harm in it. From the silence of the house, she judged the servants had already retired to their quarters. The Tribbles did not expect servants to sit up for them, not even Baxter, their stern maid.

The Marquess of Ravenswood was lying in his bath in front of the fire in his room, reading a book. He did not look up when the door softly opened, assuming his valet had come back, although the marquess had told him not to enter until he rang for him.

Felicity did not see the marquess. Not expecting him to be there, she did not even look in the direction of the fireplace, but crossed to the dressing-table and studied the contents displayed on top. There were silver-backed brushes and a jewel box, lying open to display rings and pins and seals and fobs. There was a gold watch, bottles of pomade, and a pile of letters.

The marquess looked up from his book and saw Felicity picking up the top letter and beginning to read it.

He stood up, stepped out of the bath, and crossed to where she stood just as she swung about, a look of shock on her face as she saw the naked, dripping-wet marquess.

She let out a small scream as he grasped her arm.

"What the deuce do you think you are doing? Spying on me? Reading my letters?" He gave her a shake.

"I thought it was Miss Amy's room," lied Felicity.

"You did no such thing!"

"My lord," said Felicity, closing her eyes. "You are naked."

"So I am. Do you know what is likely to happen to you if you go about prowling around gentlemen's bedrooms?"

Felicity was tired of feeling guilty. "No," she said crossly, opening her eyes and glaring at him defiantly.

"This," he said, jerking her against him. Felicity was too shocked to cry out or protest. His hot, naked, wet body was pressed tightly against her. She could feel the water soaking through the thin muslin of her gown. She was a tall girl but he was taller still. His eyes glinted wickedly down at her in the candle-light. A log fell in the fireplace and flames shot up and his wet body gleamed red in the light of the dancing flames.

"Please let me go," said Felicity with dignity. But her mouth trembled, that mouth that was too generous for fashion but promised more passion that any primped-up little rosebud.

He bent his head and kissed her, his mouth firm and cool against her own. Shock kept her passive in his arms. His lips caught fire and suddenly Felicity and the marquess were fused hotly and wetly together. With a heroic effort the marquess surfaced from a boiling sea of passion to find he was disgracefully aroused, and that if he let her go, she might see it and it might shock her out of her wits. Of course, she could *feel* it, but then he could only hope, in her innocence, she did not know what it was. As she shook and trembled in his arms, he looked wildly over his shoulder to where a fleecy towel hung on a rack near the fire. Still holding her, he waltzed her over to it, released her, swung about, grabbed the towel and knotted it about his middle.

"Get out of here!" he shouted.

And Felicity ran.

She locked herself into her room, and then sat by the fire, hugging her trembling and burning body. It was a long time before she calmed down.

But when she did so, a little smile began to curve her lips.

For the Marquess of Ravenswood had behaved every bit as shockingly as she had done herself. That comforted her for a while, until she remembered the feel of his lips and the hard feel of his body against her own.

She rose and looked at herself in the looking-glass, at her dishevelled hair and strangely swollen lips.

"Slut!" said Lady Felicity fiercely to her reflection. "Complete and uttermost *slut!*"

"Have you noticed a certain atmosphere in this house?" demanded Amy, striding up and down.

"No, I have not," said Effy crossly. "You have too much imagination, Amy."

The sisters were waiting in the drawing-room for Felicity before going to Almack's. Effy was furious at Amy's appearance. For Amy had surrendered to Yvette's wishes and was wearing one of the French dressmaker's designs. It was of green-and-gold brocade and cleverly trimmed with gold fringe to give Amy a bust where she really had none and hips where she had none either. On her head was a gold taffeta turban ornamented with a topaz brooch. She looked very grand, and Effy's nose was quite put out of joint. She herself was dressed in thin, rose-coloured silk, having insisted that Yvette make the gown to her, Effy's, design. It had little puffed sleeves out of which Effy's arms appeared like white sticks. On her head was a nut-brown wig that made her appear older than her own cloud of silver hair would have done.

Amy poured herself a glass of port and downed it in one gulp. "I tell you, Effy," she said, "something happened last night when we were at the concert. Ravenswood saw Felicity this afternoon when she was going out driving with us and he looked deuced uncomfortable and Felicity blushed to the roots of her hair, but her body seemed to go all soft and yielding. I don't like it. She ain't tamed yet, not by a long chalk, and if Ravenswood queers our pitch by throwing his leg over, I'll never forgive him."

"Lord Ravenswood would never dream of doing such a thing," gasped Effy.

"The properest of gentlemen'll do anything once their passions are roused," said Amy. "Look at Byron and Lady Caroline Lamb."

"Lord Ravenswood is not a poet. Poets are not to be trusted," said Effy primly. "Shh! Felicity is coming."

But it was the Marquess of Ravenswood who walked into the room. He was looking very fine in black evening coat and black silk breeches. His cravat was intricately tied and a large sapphire shone from amongst its snowy folds. His fair hair gleamed like newly minted guineas. As he walked to the fireplace, Amy studied the ripple of hard thigh muscle revealed by the skin-tight breeches and let out a faint sigh.

"Where is that girl?" asked the marquess. "I want this evening over and done with. I should never have promised to go. Miss Andrews is quite upset by my desertion of her."

"But it was very kind of you," said Effy, "for if you dance with Felicity, it will make her the fashion."

"I doubt if I have the power of a Brummell," he said with a reluctant smile. "But where is the tiresome child?"

Effy flashed a triumphant look at Amy. No man interested in a woman would refer to her as a tiresome child.

The door opened and Felicity walked in.

Effy noticed the hooded brooding look on the marquess's face and her heart sank. She resolved to have a sharp word with Mamselle Yvette. There was such a thing as being *too* clever with the needle. Felicity was wearing a pale-pink silk gown with an overdress of pink tissue embroidered with gold. The bodice of the dress had been cleverly cut to reveal the deep V between Felicity's excellently rounded breasts. It was of the new short length and showed tantalizing glimpses of ankle. Her masses of thick black hair had been dressed in a Roman style and ornamented with pink silk roses. She moved differently, too. The almost gawky, abrupt movements she had had when she had first come to London had admittedly been schooled away by a teacher in etiquette and a dancing master, but there was a new suppleness to her body, a new sensuousness. Effy began to wonder anxiously whether there might be something in what Amy had said.

But when they reached Almack's, both sisters' worries

disappeared. Felicity behaved beautifully and was surrounded by a group of courtiers and without any help from the marquess. The gentlemen did not seem to find her beauty unfashionable.

The marquess watched her success with a cynical eye, feeling sure all this charming behaviour of Felicity's was merely an act. He would have been very surprised had he been able to know that Felicity was deeply grateful to the gentlemen who paid her compliments. She thought they were the kindest men in the world and not what she had been led to believe about London bucks. The marquess had decided to waltz with her once and then take his leave and escape to his club.

"You see," hissed Effy behind her fan, "Ravenswood's only interest in Felicity is a desire to please *us.*"

"You are probably right," said Amy. "After all, I know almost nothing about gentlemen. And neither do you," she added waspishly.

Effy began to sob, and, conscience-stricken, Amy began to apologize and so they did not see the Marquess of Ravenswood lead Felicity onto the floor.

The dance was the waltz, which had finally been sanctioned by Almack's. He placed his arm at her waist and all at once the ballroom went away and he was back in his bedroom and he was wet and naked and he had Felicity in his arms.

He realized she was staring up at him in a stunned way and that he had pulled her against him. He muttered an excuse and held her the regulation twelve inches from him.

"Say something," said Felicity crossly, "and stop looking down your nose at me as if I am a bad piece of meat. The reason for this dance, my lord, is to secure my social success."

He smiled into her eyes and she caught her breath.

"You do not need my help," he said softly. "You already are a success."

"I hope nothing gets out about my elopement," said Felicity in a low voice. "I am not used to being a success with the gentlemen and I must confess to enjoying the novelty."

"Bremmer will not talk," he said. "Why should he? If he tattled, he would have to marry you."

A shadow crossed her face.

"Do not look sad," he said quickly. "He is only a boy. Too young for you."

For some reason that remark made Felicity feel gloriously happy and she floated round the floor in his arms.

"No, there's nothing to worry about there," said Amy, after she had soothed Effy. "Ravenswood merely seems to have taken a liking to her. He thinks of her only as a little girl."

That night, the Marquess of Ravenswood lay awake in his bedchamber. He was very conscious that Felicity was under the same roof. He wondered if she had enjoyed her evening and almost persuaded himself it would be the correct thing to do to step along to her bedchamber and ask her. He had not been able to leave for his club after that dance with her, but had stood near the entrance, watching her, telling himself all the while it was just to see she was behaving herself.

He gave himself a mental shake. He had never held Miss Andrews as intimately and passionately as he had held Felicity. That was the problem. He would try to get Betty away from that dragon of a mother of hers so that he could make love to her. That way, Felicity would once more become a tiresome young thing instead of this seductress who kept him awake.

Chapter 8

If I speak t'ye again for six months (mark the
day!),
May you call me a fool, sir, as long as I live!
Do you think one has nothing to do but
forgive?
Delia Very Angry *(Anonymous)*

THEY ARRIVED AFTER SUNSET, and so the
magnificence of Ramillies House,
home of the Duke and Duchess of Handshire, which was
supposed to strike the first frisson of terror into the common soul of Miss Betty Andrews, was lost on her.

As it was, she was too fatigued from the journey and
too upset by the presence of the Tribbles and Lady Felicity as well to take any notice of her surroundings. Mrs.
Andrews had not been invited by the marquess's parents.
Lord Ravenswood had said firmly that the Tribbles were
chaperones enough and that his parents had neglected to
include Mrs. Andrews in their invitation.

The Tribbles were distressed for different reasons: Amy

because she felt it was a waste of valuable time during which Felicity might have been better employed attracting suitable beaux; Effy because she hated the countryside with a passion and was plagued by a niggling suspicion that Amy, despite her vehement protests to the contrary, had orchestrated the whole thing so as to remove her, Effy, from Mr. Haddon's company. Effy was convinced the nabob had formed a tendre for her and that Amy was jealous.

The lamps round the courtyard, steps, and portico of the great ducal mansion had been lit. On the steps were stationed all the stable people, and inside, in the vast hall, were ranged all the indoor staff. After being conducted to their respective rooms, the visitors were told to reassemble in the hall in half an hour, where they would be conducted to supper. The marquess went in search of his parents to tell them the party had dined en route and would prefer an early night, but the duke and duchess sent word to their son that they were unavailable and would see him at supper.

When they had gathered in the hall, the butler led the way through a sort of guard of honour of liveried footmen out of the hall, across the Bow Window Room, through the Grand Cabinet, and then through a chain of state saloons to the dining-room. An orchestra, which had been playing in the hall when they arrived, were now playing in the dining-room. The duke and duchess, as was their eccentric habit, were already there, one at either end of a long table groaning with gold plate. When the members of the party were seated, they found they were such a long distance from each other that they had to shout.

Felicity was surprised at the appearance of the marquess's parents. She had expected them both to be tall and rather grand, like their son. But the duke was small and fat and cross-looking and his duchess was equally small, though thin and cold of eye. She had a steady, unnerving stare, which she fixed first on one guest and then on the other.

The only one who appeared to brighten up was Betty Andrews. She was mentally redesigning the dining-room and shortening the table and replacing the blue morocco of the dining-room seats with petit point. Betty was secure in the knowledge that when she became mistress of all this, the duke would be dead and, if his duchess did not smartly follow him to the grave, she would be packed off to the dower house. Betty was not intimidated by Ramillies House. But she *was* intimidated by her fiancé. He had whispered in her ear in the hall that he wished to be private with her later. The gleam in his eye had told Betty he expected some love-making and she felt he might at least have waited until they were married, during which happy state women were expected to endure "all that sort of thing," as Betty described the more tender side of a relationship to herself.

She found herself wishing that there were some young gentlemen present with whom she could flirt and chatter. She had met Lord Bremmer at the play one evening and had told him of her proposed visit to Ramillies House and he had pressed her hand and had said intensely he wished he could go with her, which was all that it should be and just how a gentleman ought to behave. But the marquess never said romantical things like that. Probably because he was so old, thought Betty, feeling waspish. Still, it was worth enduring. When she was duchess, she would set about making this barn of a place comfortable. And with these thoughts Betty whiled away the suppertime and did not bother to converse with anyone.

Felicity, on the other hand, did try. She roared politely at the duchess and then at the duke. They did not shout back. They had low, carrying voices, like trained actors. Felicity wondered wildly whether, as children, they had been taught to throw their voices so that they might converse amicably down the length of their monstrous dinner-table.

At last the duchess rose to her feet to lead the ladies to the drawing-room. The orchestra packed up their instruments and followed along, to reassemble themselves outside the door of the drawing-room. There was a large fire burning in the marble fireplace and the room was very warm. The walls were hung in peach-blossom cloth and the carpet was the same colour. The curtains were of rich purple silk, intermixed with peach-blossom sarsenet and trimmed with fringe, lacings, and tassels of gold-coloured silk. The furniture was covered with purple satin, woven to represent embroidery. The duchess drew Betty down on a sofa next to her and flashed a cold look at the Tribbles and Felicity, as if to warn them to keep clear.

"Tell me, Miss Andrews," said the duchess, "how you prepare rose-water?"

Betty blinked. She belonged to the new generation who allowed the servants to do everything and never went near the still-room.

"I do not know, your grace," she said, stifling a yawn and glancing at the clock.

"But you do know how to prepare cordials and medicines?"

"No, your grace. Mama has an excellent still-room maid."

"That will not answer," said the duchess severely. "You must learn. It is the first duty of every lady. I shall teach you myself." She raised an imperious hand and a footman came forward with several enormous ledgers, which he placed on a low table in front of them.

The duchess opened the ledger on the top of the pile

and extracted a piece of paper. "I wish you to observe these rules, Miss Andrews."

Betty looked dismally at a list of rules and began to read.

"The Servants are all to dine at one o'clock before the parlour Dinner, both Upper- and Under-Servants, and to Breakfast and Sup at nine. *No hot dinners,*

"The Butler or Groom of the Chambers to see that the Servants' Hall, and Powder Room, are cleaned and locked up every night before eleven o'clock.

"The plate to be washed by the Still-room Maid and in the Still-room, whence the Under-Butler must fetch it."

Betty read on through the long list, which ended up, "Should any objections be made to these rules, *those* persons may retire."

"Now," said the duchess, "I wish you to study this first housekeeping book and tell me of any economies you can suggest."

Poor Betty felt it was like being back at school. She bent her head over the ledger and prayed that the marquess and the duke would not stay long over their wine.

"And you, Lady Felicity," commanded the duchess. "Come here and take this other book and see what economies you can suggest."

Felicity looked amused. "I would not dare, your grace," she said. "I am sure you have done all that is necessary. We are all fatigued after our journey, and you cannot possibly expect any of us to enjoy household mathematics at this hour."

"Quite right," said the duchess, looking surprised. The books were taken away just as the marquess and the duke entered the room.

Betty was now beginning to feel as out of place as the duchess had hoped she would. She envied Felicity's easy dismissal of the household accounts but knew that she could never have brought herself to say such a thing. If only Ravenswood would press her hand or look at her with adoring eyes. But he was prosing on about fields and phosphates.

The Tribbles were talking quietly to each other. Amy was daring Effy to be the first to rise and say they must go to bed, and Effy was daring Amy. Then Amy noticed a spider climbing up a picture frame and said she thought it would reach the top in fifty seconds. Effy said a minute, and both sisters agreed the loser should propose retiring to bed to the duchess.

Amy took a watch like a turnip out of her reticule and began to count softly. The spider stopped its climb and hesitated.

"Go on, you fool," roared Amy suddenly.

The others fell silent. Amy turned as red as a beetroot.

"You said something?" queried the duchess frostily.

"It is very late, your grace," said Felicity. "I fear Miss Amy had fallen asleep and was having a nightmare."

"Then go to bed . . . all of you," said the duchess huffily. "Not you, Charles," she added, detaining her son.

The marquess held open the door of the drawing-room for the ladies. He pressed a note into Betty's hand.

When Betty reached her room, she opened the note and looked at it gloomily. It read, "Meet me on the terrace in front of the Grecian Room in an hour's time. R."

Betty felt tired and miserable. He should not expect her to wait up. She was exhausted. Tears filled her eyes. She wanted her mother. Felicity, now, would have known how to cope. She would no doubt send back a note saying, "Gone to sleep. Don't be silly," or something forthright like that.

Then let Felicity cope, thought Betty maliciously. They had all been crowded in the doorway when he pressed that note into her hand. Let him think he had given it to

Felicity by mistake. All Betty's jealousy of Felicity had gone. On the journey, the marquess had barely said a word to the girl and it was obvious that not only did he have no interest in her, but that he actively disliked her.

Betty knew that Felicity had the room next to her own. Her maid came in to prepare her for bed, and as soon as the woman had finished her duties and retired, Betty darted out into the corridor and slid the note under Felicity's door. Felicity would probably be asleep. The note would lie there until the morning. She, Betty, would tell the marquess in the morning when he asked where she had been that she had not received any note.

Felicity was not asleep. She was sitting reading when the note suddenly appeared. She read it and her eyebrows rose in amazement. Then she thought that Ravenswood was probably terrified she would tell Betty about that scene in his bedchamber and wished to be reassured. Well, she would torment him a little to pay him back for his bearish treatment of her on the journey. She had been longing to have an opportunity of telling him how much she detested him and now she had it.

The marquess had had difficulty in escaping from his parents and he was weary of defending Betty. "No character and no breeding," they had complained. As he hurried in the direction of the Grecian Room, he pulled out his watch and studied it in the light of an oil lamp. It was well over the hour. He hoped she had waited for him.

A full moon shone through the long windows of the Grecian Room, shining on Ionic columns and on the floor of Sienna marble. He opened the long window and walked out onto the terrace. The night was very quiet and still. The lawns rolled smoothly down in front of the terrace to a sheet of ornamental water. There was a scent of lilac in the air, mixed with the piny smell of the evergreens by the lake.

He waited and waited. He wondered what on earth was keeping the girl. He wanted to prove to himself that the searing passion he had felt for Felicity was only the result of a long period of celibacy. Betty Andrews was beautiful and dainty, all that a man could desire.

A dark bank of cloud covered the moon, plunging the terrace into thick darkness. He heard a soft movement behind him and swung about.

Felicity had spent some time trying to find the Grecian Room and had at last come across a little lamp boy who had directed her. She had a gauzy gold scarf wound about her hair. The marquess saw the faint glimmer of gold and took it for Betty's blond hair.

Felicity opened her mouth to speak as he wound his arms about her waist, but he felt for her chin and pushed her face up and sank his lips into her own. The marquess's mind dimly registered that she must be standing on something, for Betty Andrews was small in stature, but passion then clouded his reason and senses. Felicity, shocked and stunned, heard the mumbled endearments between the searing kisses and thought with a sharp stab of pure rapture that he loved her. And so she kissed him back with great enthusiasm and energy, adding fuel to the already raging fire. The increasing intimacies felt so right that all Felicity did was accommodate her throbbing body to his searching hands.

He had just prized one delectable white bosom free from its moorings in the neck of her gown and was bending his head to kiss it when Felicity sighed, "Oh, Charles."

Her voice was clear and distinctive. Betty's soft voice was marred by a slight lisp.

His hand, instead of caressing her breast, tucked it firmly back into the neckline of the gown and his head came up. At that moment the moon sailed out from behind the clouds. It was not Betty Andrews standing on some piece of masonry but Lady Felicity Vane, her eyes great dark pools in the moonlight.

"Good God," said the marquess. "I thought you were Miss Andrews."

The slap Felicity gave him nearly sent him flying off the terrace. He reeled and regained his balance, but she had gone.

Felicity lost her way in her flight through the great house until, tired of searching for her room and feeling sick with shame and exhausted with emotion, she curled up on a sofa in one of the saloons and went to sleep. The marquess went straight to her room, but did not find her. Instead he found his note to Betty lying open on Felicity's toilet table.

But he was sure he had pressed it into Betty's hand. He could not go to sleep until Felicity was found. He had behaved disgracefully. Where was she now? He wanted to ask the Tribbles for help but feared he might scandalize them. He went downstairs and back out into the grounds, searching and searching, becoming more frantic as the sky began to grow light. At last, he returned to the house and began to search through all the great rooms, which were beginning to glow red in the rising sun.

He found her in the Yellow Saloon in the west wing. She was tightly curled up on a sofa and fast asleep.

He sat down on the edge of the sofa and shook her shoulder. "Felicity!"

She came awake immediately and looked up at him, her eyes wide with fright and disgust.

"I am sorry. So very, very sorry," he said. "That note was meant for Miss Andrews. My dear Lady Felicity, I would not have dreamt of . . . How came you by that note?"

"It was pushed under my door," said Felicity.

"But I pressed it into Miss Andrews' hand as she left the drawing-room!"

"Then perhaps she knew what was in store for her," said Felicity.

"What you must think of me," he said, burying his head in his hands.

Felicity surveyed his bent head with great irritation. For one dizzy moment on the terrace, she had thought he loved her. She must have been mad. Why should she want this pompous and overbearing man to love her?

"Oh, go away," she said sharply. "Does no one get any sleep in this house?"

"But, Lady Felicity . . ."

Felicity stood up and looked down at him. Her expression was haughty and he could not help feeling their roles had been reversed. "If you think I shall tell Miss Andrews of your behaviour, you are mistaken," said Felicity. "Now conduct me to my room."

He rose immediately and offered his arm, which she ignored. He tried again.

"My behaviour was terrible, Lady Felicity," he said in a low voice. "You must forgive me."

"We shall go on as if nothing had happened," said Felicity. "How long is this visit going to be? You have taken me away from my Season."

"Only a week."

"A week!" echoed Felicity in a hollow voice. "I shall mark off the days on the wall of my room like a prisoner. I cannot understand what your parents were about to insist I and the Tribbles came too."

"They consider it most odd of me to reside with the Tribbles when I have a Town house of my own, or could use theirs."

"And how did you explain that?"

"I have not yet had an opportunity."

"And what will you say when you do have an opportunity?"

"How the devil do I know? I was sorry for the Tribbles and realized they had a difficult task with you, and so . . ."

His voice trailed away. "Worse and worse," mocked Felicity. They had reached her bedroom door. She walked inside and closed the door in his face.

The duchess did not believe people should lie in bed in the morning, eating breakfast in their rooms, and so it was a cross and sleepy party who assembled round the table in the morning-room at nine o'clock.

Effy kept glancing anxiously at Felicity. The girl was too pale and had shadows under her eyes. She hoped Felicity was not going to fall ill. What if she had caught some terrible sickness and should waste away and she and Amy would be blamed for it? The coffin lay on the hearse pulled by four coal-black horses. The mutes wailed dismally. Lady Baronsheath was distraught. "It is all your fault, Effy Tribble," she cried. And so to the graveside. The earth rattled on the coffin and the wind soughed through the old elms in the churchyard.

"Oh, it is all too much," cried Effy, bursting into tears.

"What ails you, woman?" snapped the little duchess.

"Poor Felicity," sobbed Effy. "Died so young."

Amy realized her sister had wandered into the grip of one of her fantasies and kicked her under the table. Effy yelped and started up and her elbow caught the teapot and sent the contents flying over the snowy cloth.

"You silly bitch," howled Amy. "Now look what you've done. Oh, don't cry, Effy," she added in a softer voice. "It's a bastard of a teapot anyway and made to be knocked over. A pox on these newfangled things. Bad cess to them."

"You," said the duchess awfully, "need your mouth washed out with soap."

"Sorry," said Amy. She saw Effy was blindly scrabbling about to find something to dry her streaming eyes and obligingly put a corner of the tablecloth into her shaking hands. Effy seized it gratefully and raised it to her eyes, sending teacups and plates scattering. Footmen ran about, fielding cup and saucers and mopping up tea. Felicity began to laugh and the marquess laughed as well. Betty Andrews looked from one to the other and wondered what on earth they could find so funny about this horribly embarrassing scene.

When things were restored to normal, Effy said in a shaky voice, "You are looking so white and tired, Lady Felicity, I was afraid for you."

"Of course I am looking tired," said Felicity, helping herself to coffee while the butler made more tea. "It seems we are not allowed to rest in this mansion."

"No stamina, that's your trouble," said the duke.

"I have plenty of stamina," said Felicity, suddenly deciding she did not care whether the marquess's parents liked her or not, "but I am not made of iron."

The duke turned a dangerously purple colour.

"Felicity!" cried Amy. "Apologize this minute."

"I only spoke the truth," said Felicity calmly. "It is not my behaviour which is odd. What is more odd than to chivvy your guests with the household ledgers for half the night and then roust them out of bed at this ungodly hour?"

"I have just one thing to say to you, pert miss," said the duchess awfully, "and that is . . . Oh, what is it, Giles?"

The butler coughed apologetically. "Lord Bremmer has arrived, your grace."

"Bremmer? I never asked him."

"Lord Bremmer says his carriage has broken down at our gates."

"Then take the young jackanapes and give him tea in the study and send the blacksmith down to repair his carriage."

Amy noticed that Betty's eyes, which had begun to sparkle, now held a disappointed look. She did not want the marquess to marry Betty. Perhaps this might be a way of turning Betty's affections away from the marquess. She had noticed the way the young lord had hung about Betty at the play and how he had avoided Felicity.

"I know Bremmer," she said casually. "Why not ask him to join us, your grace?"

"Oh, very well," said the duchess. "I met him two years ago and he seemed a very pleasant and prettily behaved young man, not at all like some of the rude young people one finds today." With this she cast a look of loathing on Felicity, who smiled sweetly back and helped herself to more toast.

Lord Bremmer was ushered in. His eyes went straight to Betty, who blushed and looked down at her hands. "I am most sorry, your grace," he said to the duke. "My carriage simply fell apart." He thought of all the trouble he had gone to to break it himself and hoped the sabotage would not be too obvious.

Lord Bremmer then stood helplessly wondering where he could sit down. Felicity was staring at him in a way he did not like, and the marquess was giving him a warning look. A footman came forward with a chair and Betty moved her seat sideways so that Lord Bremmer could sit next to her.

Amy began to talk loudly about Walter Scott's latest poem, saying she did not like it and had heard Scotland was a place full of savages. The duke, who had property in Scotland, protested hotly. The marquess said he had once emulated Boswell and Dr. Johnson and had journeyed as far as the Hebrides. Amy and Felicity began to question him on his travels and Lord Bremmer talked to Betty in a low voice, bringing that sparkle back to her eyes and colour to her cheeks.

But both colour and sparkle fled as breakfast finished and the marquess said, "Come for a stroll in the grounds with me, Miss Andrews."

Amy looked sharply at Felicity, but that young lady was looking unconcerned.

Betty trotted silently at the marquess's side, wishing he would not take such long steps. He led her through the Orange Grove, where orange trees stood in tubs against a hedge of laurel, and then to a conservatory at the end and ushered her in. It was full of rare plants in circular beds. Two recesses painted to look like marble held comfortable sofas where visitors could recline in the warmth of the glasshouse and study the plants.

As the marquess led the unresisting Betty to one of these sofas, she was suddenly reminded of a visit to the dentist. Her mother had taken her a year ago to have a back tooth drawn. She remembered the sinking feeling in her stomach and her attempt to pretend she was somewhere else entirely until the ordeal was over.

She sat down on a sofa and he sat beside her and took her hand in his. He looked very handsome, she tried to tell herself. "We have never been alone since the announcement of our engagement," said the marquess.

"No," whispered Betty.

"What happened last night? And how did Felicity come by the note meant for you?"

"I lost it," lied Betty. "One of the servants must have picked it up and put it under Felicity's door."

"That sounds highly unlikely," he said. "All my parents' servants know you are my fiancée."

"Perhaps they thought it was my room," said Betty desperately.

"Are you sure you did not put it there yourself?" asked the marquess.

"No," said Betty with all the sudden fury of the truly guilty. "Is that why you brought me here . . . to lecture me?"

He smiled at her suddenly. "No, my sweeting, I brought you here to kiss you, as I have been longing to do since the day I met you."

He bent his mouth to hers. Betty primmed up her lips and closed her eyes.

He tried very hard to conjure up even just a bit of that passion he had felt when he held Felicity in his arms, but he felt nothing. He tried harder, forcing her head back and kissing her savagely, and holding her in a crushing grip, almost as if he were trying to wring some passion out of her.

When he finally raised his head, she said in a shaky voice—rather the same voice she had used to the dentist—"Is it over? Can I go now?"

"Yes," said the marquess bleakly. "I am sorry if I alarmed you."

"You were very fierce and you *hurt* me," said Betty, close to tears.

"Come," he said softly, "and I will take you back to the house. You are too beautiful to be so distressed."

Betty brightened immediately, and rapped him playfully on the arm with her fan.

"You are a great brute," she said, "and you must promise your Betty never, ever to behave in such a cruel way again."

"I promise," he said. "Perhaps we are not suited."

"Oh, now you are being terribly cruel," said Betty, bursting into tears. "You don't want me to be a duchess."

"Hardly," he said drily, "since making you a duchess would mean the death of my father. Dry your eyes."

Lord Bremmer, peering through the laurel hedge, watched the couple return. He heard Betty's gulping sobs and thought that Ravenswood was the biggest brute in the world—almost as brutish as Lady Felicity Vane!

Chapter 9

"No, no; for my virginity,
When I lose that," says Rose, "I'll die";
"Behind the elms last night," cried Dick,
"Rose, were you not extremely sick?"
    Matthew Prior, A True Maid

DESPITE HIS MOTHER'S INSISTENCE that the good weather would not last, the marquess went ahead with preparations to take the small party out on the lake. The duchess protested that the joint of her big toe on her left foot was never wrong and it was now throbbing at such a rate that it could only mean a storm.

But as if to prove her big toe wrong, the sun continued to shine and the sky was clear blue. It was a cross and miserable party which set out for the lake. Betty was mildly comforted by Lord Bremmer's compliments, but secretly felt her mama would never forgive her if she threw away the chance of becoming a duchess. Amy and

Effy were feeling their age and suffering from lack of sleep. They had sat up for a long time during the night discussing the marquess and Felicity. Amy would have it that there was a certain attraction between them, and Effy would have it that they cordially loathed each other and that Ravenswood should be allowed to go ahead and marry Betty Andrews without any interference. Amy had a nagging pain in her lower back and Effy could feel the beginnings of a truly horrible headache coming on. She had tied her chin-strap too tight when she eventually got to bed, and it had left a red mark on her neck. Lord Bremmer was sure he loved Miss Andrews as no woman had ever been loved before. He, too, was tired from his long journey and his exertions in wrecking his own carriage. The marquess was grimly determined that life should go on, and yet he felt it would go on better if Lady Felicity Vane would take herself somewhere else. Her French dressmaker should be shot for contriving such seductive gowns which were just this side of indecency. Felicity was trying to persuade herself that she hated Ravenswood with a passion, and that was why her body behaved so peculiarly when he came anywhere near her.

The party stepped into flat-bottomed boats moored among the water-lilies. Effy trembled like a frightened steed. She would much have preferred to stay indoors. She did not mind formal gardens, but this lake surrounded by artistically wild undergrowth and foreign trees smacked too much of the untamed countryside. A deer came down to drink at the water's edge, and Effy thought it looked a terrifying and disgusting creature which ought to be in a zoo.

The marquess had meant to sit beside Betty, but he was the last to climb into one of the boats. Betty was sitting with Effy and Lord Bremmer, which left the marquess the only choice of going into the other boat with Amy and Felicity.

Servants climbed into a stout rowing-boat with hampers of champagne and cold meat and salad and rowed ahead to an island in the middle, where they were to have an al fresco meal.

Effy thought that rowing-boat looked eminently serviceable and wished herself on it instead of the flimsy craft she found herself in.

The pain at her temples was growing worse. A footman seized a long pole and the boat began to slide out over the water. She thought she saw Lord Bremmer press Miss Andrews' hand and felt she should remonstrate with him, but another wave of pain crashed about her head and she let out a whimper.

"Oh, Lord," exclaimed Amy from the other boat. "Effy's having one of her turns."

She stood up and the boat rocked perilously. The marquess called to the footmen in the boats to return to the shore, and said, "Do sit down, Miss Amy."

"But I cannot go," cried Amy. "You do not know what Effy is like when she has these attacks."

She jumped ashore as soon as the boat bumped against the bank and shrieked to the footman in Effy's boat to bring her back.

"Stop frowning and scowling, Ravenswood," said Felicity suddenly. "Miss Effy is sick and cannot go. I suggest we all return to the house."

"And I suggest we go without Miss Amy and Miss Effy," snapped the marquess.

Amy was helping her sister out of the boat and then she began to lead her away from the water. Effy did look very ill indeed. Felicity made to rise to get out of the boat herself, but the marquess shouted to the footman, "Push off, man. We haven't got all day."

The boat set off again with a jerk and Felicity collapsed back in her seat.

"Well, my lord," she said acidly. "I feel I have been kidnapped. Is this your idea of a pleasure outing?"

"It is a fine day and the water is pretty," he said.

"But you are in a bad temper and determined to spoil everyone else's pleasure," remarked Felicity.

"I am *not* in a bad temper," he said savagely and turned his head away, affording Lady Felicity a good view of his excellent profile.

"Then don't sulk," said the incorrigible Felicity.

"Do you really love him?" Lord Bremmer was whispering to Betty.

Betty blushed and hung her head. "I—I think so," she said softly, "and yet he frightens me."

"I would never frighten you," said Lord Bremmer, removing his hat so that he could toss back his curls in what he hoped was a Byronic manner. He gave her a smouldering look. "I would cherish you. You are so very delicate and beautiful, I fear you might break."

Betty sighed. If only Ravenswood would say such lovely things. She glanced across at the other boat. He was scowling fiercely and Lady Felicity was lying back against the cushions, one hand trailing in the water. Her muslin gown was embroidered with little blue cornflowers. Betty felt a pang of envy. She must try to get Mama to lure that dressmaker away from the Tribbles. Felicity was wearing one of the new "transparent" hats, a circle of gauze decorated with poppies and cornflowers and long blue satin ribbons that trailed down her back.

They arrived at the island. It was a pretty strip of land with a small artificial beach made of sand behind which was a carefully cut green crescent of lawn, surrounded by trees.

The servants had spread the picnic out on a white cloth

on the grass. The party sat down to eat and drink champagne, kept cold with ice from the ice-house. The marquess gave them a long lecture on how the ice was cut in blocks in the winter and stacked deep in the ice-house in the ground. Felicity thought he looked like a thundercloud and was not a bit surprised, for it transpired that she was sitting on one side of the cloth with Lord Ravenswood while Betty and Lord Bremmer sat on the other. Betty had placed herself next to Lord Bremmer and did not seem to realize that she should be seated next to her fiancé.

Lord Bremmer and Betty drank a great deal of champagne and chatted about various people they knew. The marquess drank steadily and silently and occasionally looked broodingly at his fiancée but did nothing to break up her conversation with Lord Bremmer.

The marquess thought of his disappointing love scene with Betty and began to wonder whether the girl's coldness and fright had been because Felicity had told her about that unfortunate accident on the terrace. Perhaps his own lack of response had been because of Betty's coldness. He became determined to ask Felicity, and when the meal was finished, dismissed the servants. Betty said she would like to walk to the end of the island where there was a white-pillared temple, a folly built by one of the Handshire ancestors. Lord Bremmer eagerly offered to escort her, blushed, and looked guiltily towards the marquess. But the marquess merely nodded in an abstracted way, so Lord Bremmer led Betty off, leaving the marquess alone with Felicity.

"Lord Bremmer is enamoured of Miss Andrews, I think," said Felicity, unpinning her hat and placing it on the grass beside her. "You should not let them be alone together."

"I shall attend to them in a minute," said the marquess,

hugging his knees and staring at the grass. "I wanted to talk to you in private."

"Good heavens! Why?"

"Did you tell Miss Andrews of that unfortunate episode last night?"

"On the terrace? Of course not. That would be cruel."

The marquess made a move as if to get up.

"Why do you ask?" demanded Felicity. Her heart had lifted when he had said he wanted to talk privately to her. Disappointment that the only reason he wanted to be alone with her was to be reassured that his monstrous behaviour had not reached the delicate ears of his fiancée, who must be cherished and protected unlike such a hurly-burly girl as herself, enraged her. There was no pleasing anyone. Her father had wanted her to be a boy, and so she had tried to the best of her ability to be as boyish as possible. Now her mother wanted her to charm some man into marriage, and she could not oblige her and get on with it because she was stuck down in the country with this heartless satyr.

"There was a certain coldness in her treatment of me," he said.

"Dear, dear," mocked Felicity. "You probably mauled her the way you mauled me last night."

"*What!*"

"I said, you probably mauled her the way you mauled me last night."

"I did not maul you. I made love to you under the impression you were Miss Andrews."

"Mauled me! Mauled me!" jeered Felicity. "You with your great, hot, greasy, *disgusting* hands!"

"How dare you, you jade!"

"In fact," went on Felicity in a maddeningly cool voice, "if you want to get Miss Andrews to the altar, then I

142

suggest you do not try to subject her to the intimacies of the bedchamber beforehand. Faugh!"

He leaned towards her threateningly. "Why so faint and disgusted now, Miss Prim? As I recall, you returned my caresses."

"I was humouring you. You are quite, quite mad."

There came a growling rumble of thunder from the west, but the marquess paid it no heed.

"You are a spoilt brat," said the marquess, raising his voice even higher as the grumbling of thunder grew louder.

"And you are a fool," said Felicity. "I can guess what happened. You were horrified that such as I could rouse you to passion. You are the sort of fellow who thinks one woman is the same as another. And so you made love to her and nothing happened and now you are taking your frustration and spite out on me."

"Oh, I apologized for my behaviour," he said. "I admit I became carried away, but I was very tired and I think the wine at dinner must have gone to my head."

"Perhaps you have the right of it," said Felicity in a suddenly calm voice. "I am sure many men could rouse such a response. I must start experimenting right away as soon as we return to London."

He rolled over towards her and grasped her arms and forced her back on the grass. "Listen," he said between his teeth, "you have caused the Tribbles enough pain and anguish. You will behave!"

"You are hurting me!"

"And I will hurt you a lot more if you persist in your wild ways."

A tremendous crack of lightning split the sky. Felicity looked over his shoulder at the boiling purple clouds that had suddenly appeared over their heads.

She wriggled in an effort to free herself. "Let me go! We shall be soaked to the skin."

Her face was flushed and her hair was tumbled about her face.

The anger died out of his eyes and he looked down at her in dawning surprise.

She looked up into his eyes, and then her gaze fell to his firm lips. Her body felt hot and heavy.

Lightning flashed again and rain began to drum down upon them.

He felt her breasts pressed against his chest and he could smell the light flower perfume she wore.

Approaching screams heralded the return of Betty and Lord Bremmer. The marquess released Felicity and said quietly, "We had better get to the boats."

He helped her to her feet and they turned to face the dripping spectacle of Betty Andrews, who was being helped towards them by Lord Bremmer.

A great clap of thunder shook the heavens and Betty tripped forward and threw herself into the marquess's arms. "I am so frightened," she said.

"Come along," he said, putting an arm about her waist. He called over his shoulder, "The servants have gone back, Bremmer. I hope you can manage the boat."

Lord Bremmer and Felicity looked at each other, rain pouring down their cheeks like tears.

Then they made their way to one of the boats while the marquess helped Betty into the other.

As Lord Bremmer pushed off with the long pole, Felicity picked up a scoop and began to bail rain-water from the boat. With clumsy, inexpert pushes with the pole, Lord Bremmer propelled them towards the middle of the lake. Another long fork of lightning striking down unnerved him. He gave the pole an extra-hard thrust and it stuck fast in the mud. The boat and Felicity sailed on, leaving Lord Bremmer up the pole like a monkey. "Help!" he screamed. "I can't swim!" Then pole and Lord Bremmer fell in the water.

Nearby, Betty's cries sounded like an echo. "Help! I can't swim." For the marquess had told Betty to bail and then had concentrated on poling the boat, not knowing that Betty had made no effort at all to obey his instructions, thinking that bailing was a job for servants. The boat had quickly filled up and had slowly begun to sink below the surface.

Lord Bremmer was gasping and screaming. Felicity dived off the boat and swam to him. Then she heard the marquess shout, "You can stand, Bremmer. It's shallow."

Felicity stood up. The water reached to her neck. She caught hold of the thrashing and plunging lord and shouted at him to stand still. Lord Bremmer floundered and staggered and stood up.

"What a fuss about nothing," laughed Felicity, and then the laughter died on her lips. Through the curtain of rain, she could see the marquess making his way towards the shore with Betty cradled in his arms. It was a tender scene.

Felicity felt cold and depressed. She waded towards the bank and then felt herself being seized and lifted out of the water. The marquess set her down, his eyes alight with laughter. "Did you ever see such a ridiculous situation, Felicity?" he said. "Both of them howling like banshees in a few feet of water."

Betty Andrews stood shivering and shaking, watching them with hate-filled eyes. All her old jealousy of Felicity had returned. Lord Bremmer had been sweet and tender and she had even let him steal a kiss. But Betty was determined to be a duchess, and Felicity was not going to get in her way.

She gave a faint moan and sank artistically on the grass

in a pretended faint. There came the sound of running feet and she felt herself seized in strong arms and raised up. She pretended to recover consciousness and opened her eyes. Lord Bremmer's face appeared above her own. "Lie still, my precious darling," he said. "I have you safe."

Betty twisted her head round his protective arm and looked back. The marquess and Felicity were walking side by side. They were both laughing helplessly.

The sheer indifference and cruelty of it made Betty feel genuinely ill.

Felicity had accused the marquess of hard-heartedness and the marquess had pointed out that Betty's faint was the best effort he had seen off the stage. It had struck them both as funny that Betty, when she pretended to recover, would find herself in Bremmer's arms and not the marquess's, though neither of them would dream of confessing such an unkind thought to the other.

The Tribbles stood side by side at the window of the downstairs drawing-room and surveyed the returning party. "She's got him!" exulted Amy, meaning Felicity had got Ravenswood. The dripping-wet couple were still laughing helplessly, each in the grip of that insane fit of giggles which only lovers and children know.

"No, she has not," said Effy quietly. "Miss Andrews is very ambitious and she wants to be a duchess one day. She will not release Ravenswood from the engagement."

"We must do something," said Amy. "Where's that duchess?"

"Why? I must say her grace proved most kind and the cordial she gave me for my headache worked almost immediately."

"Thought of something" was all Amy would say.

She strode off with great mannish strides.

To underline her fragile condition, Betty would have been happy to spend the rest of the day lying down in her darkened bedchamber. Her maid opened the door and came quietly in. Before she closed the door behind her, Betty heard the faint tinkling of a piano.

"Who is playing?" she asked sleepily.

"Lady Felicity," said the maid. "My lady is entertaining the gentlemen."

Colour flooded Betty's cheeks and she began to struggle out of bed. "Oh, she is, is she?" she muttered. "Get me dressed quickly."

Betty's idea of dressing quickly meant only an hour was allowed for pinning the gown, fastening the tapes, dressing the hair, and applying rouge to the cheeks and lips. Then there was all the agonizing business of choosing the right fan and arranging a Norfolk shawl to hang in the correct way, and then the right colour of gloves had to be found. It was all so exhausting a business that Betty sometimes wondered whether the lower orders ever realized what a tremendous amount of work a society lady had to do.

She was just about ready to leave her room when Amy walked in. Betty eyed her with disfavour. Some of the bone pins had fallen out of Amy's hair and one iron-grey lock was hanging over her face. She was wearing one of her old shabby round gowns, despite the fact that the dressmaker had made her several flattering new ones. Amy hated the waistline being up under her bust and preferred it to be where a waistline ought to be. The slim line of her new gowns did not allow her the same freedom of movement as her old ones.

"Came to see how you were," said Amy gruffly. She sat down in a chair and stuck her feet out in front of her and examined them as if she had never seen them before.

"I am much better," said Betty stiffly. "I am about to go downstairs."

"Devil of a business finding one's way about this barn,"

said Amy. "I admire your courage. Terrible thing being a duchess and having to run all this. Of course, that might not happen for a long time. Frisky is the duke. Very."

"He must be nearly sixty," said Betty impatiently.

"Tol-rol. *His* father was ninety when he died. Still, Ravenswood's got a big place of his own. He often says he don't really want to be a duke. Got half a mind to hand the succession over to his younger brother Harry, the one who's at the wars."

"He would never do that."

"Oh, he just might," said Amy. "He doesn't appear to pay much heed to his parents, but the fact is he dotes on them. Now the duchess was saying to him that she did not think you had it in you to manage Ramillies House, and I could see that was worrying him. He says to her, he says, 'Don't worry, Mama. I am sure Harry will find the proper duchess for you.' "

"I have never heard of such a thing!" gasped Betty.

"It happens," said Amy laconically. "Look at the Marquess of Drent. He turned down the dukedom in the last century."

"I know about that," said Betty impatiently. "But Drent was mad."

"Exactly," said Amy cheerfully.

"You mean . . . ? I don't believe you. There is no madness in Ravenswood's family."

"You ain't met his Aunt Matilda," said Amy, who really enjoyed lying once she had got into her stride. "Thinks she's Queen Elizabeth. But if you're set on marrying him and getting to be a duchess one day, you'd better start convincing this duchess that you're suitable for the job. Ask her advice. Get her to show you around. Ravenswood'll love that."

"If you will excuse me," said Betty stiffly. "I wish to go downstairs."

Amy watched her leave and then got to her feet. "I hope she's taken the bait," she murmured to herself. "Now to find Effy and hatch out a way of making her think Ravenswood is mad."

"I'm in love with him and I want him for myself! There!" said Lady Felicity Vane to her own reflection. She heaved a great sigh of relief. She had admitted it at last. But there was no hope. Betty was pleasing the little duchess greatly and was to be seen dutifully scurrying after her from cellar to attic, examining linen, quizzing servants on their duties, and working in the still-room. Ravenswood had become cold and distant and formal and Lord Bremmer had become more Byronic than ever—Byronic, that is, in his view, but moody and sulky in everyone else's. His carriage was mended, there was no reason for him to stay, and yet stay he did.

Felicity wished she knew what the marquess was thinking.

Amy was no help. Felicity had found her muttering to herself something that sounded like "She's pleasing the duchess and I didn't think she would and he don't look a bit mad."

Felicity turned as Wanstead came into the room. "Would you please do something pretty with my hair, Wanstead?" she asked. "There is to be dancing after dinner. The duchess wants a demonstration of the quadrille."

"Beg pardon, my lady?"

Felicity realized she had spoken in her normal voice. Wanstead was slightly deaf and could be very deaf if she did not want to hear anything. Felicity repeated what she had just said in a loud voice.

"Of course I will," said Wanstead. "Sit down at the toilet table, my lady, and I'll do my best."

Felicity smiled. "I don't know what's come over you, Wanstead. You always do my hair so well these days. I almost forget the times you used to try to yank the hair out of my head."

"Perhaps," said Wanstead, "it's because of the change in you, my lady. You say 'please' and 'thank you' these days and it makes you a pleasure to work for."

"Have I been such a monster?" asked Felicity ruefully.

"Yes, my lady," said Wanstead. "Now do be quiet and let me work."

"So," finished Amy, "all my manipulating gone for nothing. Her grace has just informed me that Betty Andrews is a treasure."

"You should have consulted me," said Effy severely. "You are too impetuous, Amy."

"Well, I am usually more direct than you," said Amy hotly. "I always go to the heart of the matter."

"Then go to the heart of the matter," said Effy maliciously. "Go and tell Ravenswood he's in love with Felicity and you want him to behave like a madman to release him from his engagement."

Amy looked at her sister with her mouth open. Then she laughed. "Bless me, you've got it, Effy," she crowed and gallumphed out of the room, slamming the door behind her.

By diligently questioning the servants, Amy found the marquess had gone out riding. She was so impatient to find him that she went straight to the stables and demanded a horse. The head groom fussed about, saying he must look for a side-saddle, but Amy roared at him that she could manage to ride with an ordinary saddle. Soon she was galloping off on a huge mount, her large feet stuck in the stirrups and her skirts hitched up to reveal scarlet stockings.

The marquess had ridden over to the Home Farm and had just completed his visit when he saw Amy flying towards him. He had a sudden sinking feeling in his stomach. There must be something up with Felicity to make Amy Tribble ride hell for leather like that. Amy came galloping up, reined in her horse, and tumbled out of the saddle to stand beside him.

"My lord," she gasped. "You must appear mad as soon as possible."

"Why? What has happened?"

"You must give Miss Andrews a disgust of you as soon as possible," said Amy.

"What on earth are you talking about?"

"You must break your engagement to Miss Andrews, or rather, force her to break it."

"You make me feel incredibly stupid," said the marquess patiently, "but I still do not have the faintest idea what you mean."

Amy sighed and then said carefully, "You, Ravenswood, are madly in love with Felicity. You don't want to marry Miss Andrews. She is ambitious and won't release you unless you do something about it. I told her there was madness in your family, but I don't think she believed me."

"I am beginning to think there is madness in *your* family, Miss Tribble. I do not love Lady Felicity."

"Pish, man, I am not blind."

The marquess stood looking at the ground. He stood in silence for a long time. Then he said slowly, "Do not worry, Miss Amy, I am well able to handle my own affairs."

"But . . ."

"No, you must not interfere. Not another word. Come

along and I will ride back with you. We have only a half-hour left in which to change for dinner."

The Duchess of Handshire was not entirely insensitive. She prided herself on her table and wondered what had happened to everyone's appetite. Moody silence reined and the guests picked at their food, with the exception of Amy, who cheerfully ate everything on her plate.

Betty looked as pretty as ever, although there were slight shadows under her eyes. Felicity had an abstracted air and drank too much, and for once Effy had not the heart to chide her. Lord Bremmer kept sending smouldering looks in the direction of Betty and kept asking her to take wine with him throughout the meal.

When they were all assembled in the drawing-room, they stood about talking. The marquess took Betty off into a corner and began to speak to her intensely. Amy brightened at the growing look of horror on Betty's face and wondered what he was saying.

The duchess commanded a demonstration of the quadrille. Effy sat down to play. Not one of them performed very well and the demonstration came to an abrupt end when Lord Bremmer attempted an entrechat and twisted his ankle.

Felicity thought the evening would never end. They were to leave on the morrow. Ravenswood had hardly spoken to her, and when he looked at her, his expression was veiled. There was no hope. Her head felt heavy. She would make amends to her mother for her previous wildness by marrying quietly and suitably. The idea was so depressing that she felt tears beginning to prick at the back of her eyes.

It was a sorry group that set out the next day on the long road back. Only Effy became visibly brighter as streets and shops began to appear on either side. Felicity was wishing the marquess would take himself off. She felt she could not bear to be under the same roof as him and to endure visits from Betty and her mother and to listen to preparations for the wedding.

Felicity slept heavily that night, not waking until late in the morning. She went reluctantly downstairs and then heard a querulous, complaining voice raised in the drawing-room.

Mrs. Andrews.

Felicity felt she could not bear it. She retreated to her room, dived into bed, fully clothed, and pulled the blankets over her head.

Downstairs in the drawing-room, the amazed Tribble sisters and the Marquess of Ravenswood were listening to a lecture from Mrs. Andrews.

"I could not believe my ears," that lady was saying. "My poor little darling is quite, quite shattered. All that divine beauty to be so persecuted. The duchess making her slave from morning to night over the housekeeping as if my lambkin were a scullery maid. Nasty smelly messes in the still-room! And you!" Mrs. Andrews rounded on the marquess. "You *monster!*"

"I?" demanded the marquess, giving her a limpid look.

"Yes, you. You told Betty you wanted twenty children in quick succession and that she would never come to Town because you intended to spend the rest of your days in the country. You said you wanted a meek and biddable wife and did not hold with ladies spending money on gowns. Three gowns a year you said was enough," said Mrs. Andrews, her voice rising to a scream. "Well, let me tell you this: I should have known what you were like, Ravenswood, when you took up residence with these two frights. Betty tells me there is madness in your family. So, hear this! I, myself, went straight to the newspapers this very morning and put in a notice cancelling your engagement. And what have you to say to that?"

"Thank you," said the marquess with a low bow. "Of course, my heart is broken."

"Fiddle," said Mrs. Andrews. "You haven't got a heart. Lord Bremmer has a heart. Betty said if it weren't for him you would have left her fainting in the middle of a thunderstorm to die of pneumonia. Good day to you all, and I hope I never see any of you again!"

She departed in a flurry of purple silk and strong scent.

"My stars!" cried Effy. "I was beginning to think nothing would work."

"My dear Miss Amy, my dear Miss Effy," said the marquess. "May I have your permission to . . . ?"

"Get along with you," said Amy, grinning like a schoolboy. "She's in her room."

Felicity heard the door opening but kept her eyes tightly closed. She thought it was probably one of the sisters, come to summon her to the drawing-room, and did not want to be bothered.

Someone sat on the bed. Felicity feigned a faint snore.

"Felicity," said a deep voice.

She opened her eyes and twisted round and looked up into the Marquess of Ravenswood's face.

"What do you want?" she demanded tearfully. "Are you come to plague me?"

"I am come to ask you to marry me. No one will have me. Miss Andrews' mother has cancelled the engagement."

"Why do you want to marry me?" demanded Felicity.

"I love you."

"Oh, Charles," sighed Felicity, winding her arms about his neck. "When did you know you loved me?"

"When Miss Amy Tribble told me so."

"That is not at all romantic."

"Then is this," he said softly, bending his face to hers, "and this . . . and this . . . ?"

"Oh, Charles. Kiss me again."

"Come away from that door this minute, Amy Tribble," said Effy. "You shouldn't be listening."

"I'm a chaperone, ain't I?" said Amy, pressing her ear to the panels of Felicity's bedroom door once more. "I'm the best chaperone in the world. Damme, we're both the best." She swung to face Effy, her eyes blazing. "By George, we've done it."

From inside came the creak of bedsprings. "Dear, dear," cried Effy. "We must stop them."

"I don't think Ravenswood will go too far," said Amy cheerfully. "Come along, Effy. This calls for champagne."

"We had better go and tell the Tribbles the good news," said the marquess after he had reluctantly freed his lips. "We must be married soon, for you are not safe with me."

Dizzy with passion and happiness, they made their way downstairs.

"I think they know already," said the marquess, as they paused outside the drawing-room.

From inside came the noise of Amy roaring out a chorus of "The Gay Hussar" while Effy thumped the piano keys with gusto.

"Another kiss," whispered the marquess, pulling Felicity back into his arms.

Felicity held him away. "Did you tell Betty something to frighten her away?" she asked.

"Only that I wanted twenty children."

Felicity began to laugh. "What a lovely idea," she said. "When do we start?"

He shook her and smiled down at her. "You are still wild," he said. "Come, kiss me and promise me you will never change."

Chapter 10

*Love rules the camp, the court, the grove—for
love
Is heaven, and heaven is love.*
                              —Lord Byron

LADY BARONSHEATH HAD A house guest, a Mrs. Toddy, a comfortable, cheerful widow who was gratifyingly interested in all the details of Lady Felicity's forthcoming marriage. Lady Baronsheath had worried that her husband might write from America, forbidding the wedding to take place until his return. But the earl had written he was highly delighted, callously adding he was sure his wife would see the couple spliced without his help.

The countess was to travel to London the following week to begin arrangements for the wedding in St. George's, Hanover Square. She was glad of Mrs. Toddy's easygoing company, for she feared by each post to learn that Felicity had changed her mind. She could not quite believe that her daughter was to be so respectably married, albeit the engagement was dreadfully short—a mere three months.

"What you have not told me," said Mrs. Toddy, between sips of tea, "is how you came to know the Tribble sisters, and how you came to choose them to school Felicity. It turned out a brilliant choice, but how could you guess? I know them slightly myself, and Amy Tribble is definitely odd."

Lady Baronsheath hesitated and then said, "I shall tell you if you promise not to breathe a word to a soul."

Mrs. Toddy looked suitably solemn. "Not a word shall pass my lips."

The countess took the now yellowing newspaper out of the drawer and smoothed it out and handed it to Mrs. Toddy. "I was at my wit's end," she said, "and I saw this advertisement and answered it. I did not know anything of the Tribble sisters at that time."

Mrs. Toddy read the advertisement slowly and carefully. "What an amazing thing," she said at last. "No, I will certainly not tell anyone. Everyone believes the Tribbles to be friends of yours."

Mrs. Toddy left Greenboys before Lady Baronsheath's departure to London, assuring her friend that she would most definitely attend the wedding and considered herself honoured to be included among the guests.

On her return to Tunbridge Wells, Mrs. Toddy found that Lady Baronsheath's secret had grown uncomfortably large. It was misery to have such a splendid piece of gossip and have to keep it to oneself.

She was choosing silks in a shop one afternoon when Lady Fremley, one of the residents of the spa, came in. They chatted while they inspected the silks and Lady Fremley declared herself green with envy that Mrs.

Toddy was to attend the wedding of the year. She begged Mrs. Toddy to return with her for a dish of tea.

Lady Fremley liked to lace her afternoon tea with brandy, and Mrs. Toddy soon found her tongue loosened, and she told Lady Fremley all about the Tribbles' advertisement, but swore her to secrecy.

But Lady Fremley had not such a conscience as Mrs. Toddy, and finding the secret burning inside her, she duly started to unburden herself to all and sundry until it appeared as if the whole of the upper echelons of Tunbridge Wells had been sworn to keep the secret.

And so the gossip spread out like ripples in a pool, and the little tide of murmured gossip washed up on the shores of London before Felicity's wedding. It spread quickly round the upper ranks of society and then down to the lesser ranks, the lesser ranks including Mr. Desmond Callaghan.

That Pink of the Ton was quite outraged, for all were speaking of the Tribble sisters with great admiration. He wished he had known earlier and then he might have tried to spike their guns by doing something to ruin their job as chaperones. Still, he suddenly thought, there might be a next time . . .

Amy and Effy had received a comfortable bonus of three thousand pounds from Lady Baronsheath. Effy was happily content with it. They had employed their own staff of servants and had even bought some of their own pictures for the walls, Felicity having learned at last where both pictures and servants had come from. But as the day of the wedding approached, Amy began to grow anxious. The eight thousand pounds Lady Baronsheath had given them to bring out Felicity had all gone, and now they were eating into the bonus of three thousand. Eight thousand pounds might appear a fortune to most of the population, but it was only a sufficient amount for an aristocratic Season, especially with the inflationary prices of the Regency. Although Felicity was engaged, they were still expected to chaperone her for the length of the London Season. There were so many callers to entertain and all the new servants to pay on quarter-day.

At last Amy was forced to darken Effy's spirits by confiding her worries. Effy said that she was sure Mr. Haddon was about to propose to her, Effy, but that piece of intelligence only served to send Amy into a towering passion and she accused Effy of being totally useless and living in fantasies.

Mr. Haddon arrived. "But you need not worry," he said after Effy had been soothed down and Amy had explained the problem, although Amy could not help adding nastily that Effy was living in dreams of *someone* proposing to her. Effy had looked hopefully at Mr. Haddon at this point and toyed flirtatiously with her fan, but he appeared buried in thought. She began to sniffle dismally.

"Yes," he said thoughtfully, "I do not see why you are worrying. It appears to be all over London that Lady Baronsheath answered an advertisement of yours. I am sure you will not even need to advertise for a difficult girl this time."

"But I don't want to go through all that business again," wailed Effy. "Difficult girls are so exhausting."

"Nonsense," said Amy, much cheered. She flung her new shawl about her shoulders and twisted this way and that to admire the effect. "We shall have our pick of 'em."

In Tunbridge Wells, Mr. and Mrs. Burgess sat in their dark, overfurnished drawing-room.

"It is of no use discussing these Tribble people," said

Mrs. Burgess to her husband. "It would not work with Fiona. My niece is hardened and steeped in sin."

"As far as I see it," said Mr. Burgess, rising to his feet and beginning to walk up and down, "we do not have much hope. She is a very wealthy heiress and you would think some man would want her."

"And so they did!" cried Mrs. Burgess. "Four, to be precise. And what happened? Each was left alone with her to pay his address, and all reeled out of the house without proposing, never to be heard of again. But even a whipping could not raise anything more out of Fiona except that they must have changed their minds and she did not know why. My niece is very rich and the management of her money passes out of our hands on the day she marries. I tell you, Mr. Burgess, people will begin to say it is all our fault and that we are stopping her getting married. Have we not done our best? Have we not read the Bible to her daily? Have we not kept her on bread and water?"

"If she went off to these Tribbles," said Mr. Burgess, "she would at least be out of our hands for more than a Season. Say they took her about November to start her schooling, we should be shot of her for at least eight months. It is not our money that will pay for it, but Fiona's. And I think the expense well justified. I have prayed nightly for guidance and I firmly believe God has sent news of the Tribbles to us."

Mrs. Burgess thought of eight months without Fiona.

"Very well," she said. "We shall travel to London as soon as this wedding is over and broach the matter to them. I suppose they are very expensive."

"Oh, yes," said Mr. Burgess. "Lady Fremley told Mrs. Jessop that she had had it from Mrs. Toddy that at least ten thousand pounds plus a bonus if the girl weds well is what they are demanding. I asked Mrs. Toddy, who screamed she had never breathed a word, and added that she could not have said any sum of money, for Lady Baronsheath had not mentioned money."

"Considering the amount of wealth our useless niece has, ten thousand is a mere drop," said Mrs. Burgess. "The matter is settled. Fiona shall go to the Tribbles."

Felicity had endured the wedding rehearsal. She was beginning to wonder whether to run away. The marquess was as cross as a bear, and when he had bent to kiss her at the wedding rehearsal, he had mumbled first that all this cursed to-ing and fro-ing was driving him mad and he was heartily bored with the whole thing. His lips had then descended on her own in a brief, cold kiss.

Miss Betty Andrews had become engaged to Lord Bremmer, and Felicity reflected gloomily that at least *they* looked like a couple in love. She had seen them in the Park the other day, and they had been gazing into each other's eyes. Felicity had returned to be confronted by the marquess, who had taken exception to one of the Baronsheaths' guests and had asked Felicity coldly if she would please do some of the work on the wedding herself, instead of jauntering around and leaving everyone else to cope with it.

Felicity had been as deeply hurt and wounded as only a young woman in love at the receiving end of a remark like that can be. At times she thought her mother's sheer delight in the whole business was the only thing stopping her from teaching the marquess a well-deserved lesson by crying off.

All those aching yearnings he had started up in her body were still there, and not one of them, it seemed, was to be assuaged by the slightest caress. He reminded her of her hunting friends at her coming-out ball who had all treated her like the man her father had so wanted her to be.

Other girls might dream of their honeymoons of being alone with their beloved at last, and Felicity was no exception—except that she longed to be alone with the marquess so that she could throw something at his head and then tell him exactly what she thought of him.

The day of her wedding was wet and gloomy, and Wanstead fussed about, moaning that it was a bad omen. Felicity threw a hairbrush at her, which Wanstead deftly caught and then proceeded to madden Felicity further by giving her a lecture on how some girls never reform.

Amy was too carried away by her own new outfit to notice Felicity's distress. It was a green wool gown of mannish cut, decorated with a jabot of gold lace and with a froth of gold lace at the wrists. Mr. Haddon had said she looked "very fine" and had given her a present of a fine Kashmir shawl and had begged her not to tell Effy, because the other shawls he had brought back had got the moth in them and were sadly damaged. So now Amy and Mr. Haddon had a secret that Effy was not part of, and Amy delightedly hugged the knowledge to herself and told Effy that she herself had bought the shawl from Lady Rochester. Amy blithely meant to warn Lady Rochester of the lie, but forgot in all the bustle of wedding preparations.

As Felicity sat in the drawing-room, waiting for the carriage that was to take her to the church, Mr. Haddon whispered to Effy that he thought Lady Felicity looked absolutely furious about something, but Effy was too intimidated by the presence of the earl's brother, Lord Devere, to pay much attention to anything. Lord Devere was very like the Earl of Baronsheath, being large, ebullient, and noisy.

Looking at Felicity's set face on the road to the church,

Lord Devere assumed she had bride nerves and told her several very warm stories in an effort to cheer her up. He had drunk a great deal and was very unsteady on his feet as he led her up the aisle.

Amy and Effy sat pressed close together during the service, and when the marquess said, "I do," Amy stifled a sob and clutched Effy's gloved hand. How many long and weary nights had both of them dreamt that one day one of them would be standing where Felicity now was. Both sisters gave up trying to be brave and cried dismally, and at one point Amy's wails threatened to drown the noise of the organ.

When they left the church, Amy was about to climb into their carriage to follow the happy couple to the wedding breakfast when she suddenly saw Desmond Callaghan standing in the crowd outside. He gave her such a malevolent look that Amy shivered. Then she comforted herself with the thought that there was little such a weakling could do to them.

The wedding breakfast was held at the Handshires' Town house, which had been specially opened up for the occasion, the duke and duchess preferring to spend the year round in the country.

Speeches were made and toasts were drunk and dances were danced, and then Felicity was off again with her marquess to take up her new life.

She kissed her mother and hugged Amy and Effy and climbed into the closed carriage—closed because there was a steady drizzle falling. She jerked down the window and threw out her bouquet, and with an enormous leap Amy seized it and waved it triumphantly.

Felicity smiled and waved back and then sank back in her seat.

"I have something to say to you, my lord," she said, turning and looking at the marquess.

"Thank God, that is all over," he said, taking off his hat and throwing it on the seat opposite. "What have you to say, my love? You have been looking daggers at me this age."

"How dare you bully me and treat me so coldly," raged Felicity. "If you think that is what you are going to get away with now we are married, be sure you are much mistaken. I am not frightened of you, you great oaf." And with that, she drew back her fist and punched him hard on the side of his face.

He seized her hands and held them prisoner. "I have not been cold," he said. "Goodness, all these medieval preparations were enough to drive a man mad."

"Miss Andrews is engaged and in love for all the world to see," said Felicity, struggling to free her hands. "Lord Bremmer smiles on her and dotes on her, and yet you appear hell-bent on showing everyone you do not care for me one jot."

"I want you in my bed, you silly goose. I love you and I was afraid to touch you lest I found I could not wait for our wedding. Oh, Felicity, I *ache* for you."

"Really, Charles?" asked Felicity in a mollified voice.

"Kiss me, my love, and I will show you how much." He held her close in his arms, feeling all the familiar passion she roused with a heady exaltation. Felicity's white wedding gown was embroidered with tiny seed pearls. Some began to rattle on the floor of the carriage under the strain of questing hands and heaving bodies.

They came to their senses, both blushing as they realized the carriage steps were down and a wooden-faced footman was holding open the door.

The marquess got down and brushed aside the footman and lifted Felicity in his arms and carried her into the house.

Humphrey, the butler, was standing there, looking

more pompous than ever. Humphrey knew how things should be done. Although Felicity already knew all the servants, Humphrey felt it was only correct that the new marchioness should be introduced to them all over again, and so the staff were lined up in the hall.

The butler unrolled a long piece of parchment and began his prepared speech. But he only got as far as the first sentence.

"Splendid, Humphrey," interrupted the marquess, still holding Felicity in his arms. "Good to be home. Serve champagne to the staff and give them a guinea each."

He made for the stairs.

"My lord!" called Humphrey, outraged. "I have no instructions. Do you not wish to dine?"

"No," said the marquess crossly, "we are fatigued and are going to bed."

Humphrey blushed scarlet, but mindful of his position, he tried again. "And when would my lord and my lady like breakfast?"

"Next week," called the marquess and bounded lithely up the stairs with Felicity.

He ran straight into his bedchamber, kicked the door shut behind him, and then gently placed her on her feet. He tilted up her chin and looked deep into her eyes.

"Just us," he said softly. "Just the two of us." He pulled her gently to him and kissed her on the lips. Then he smiled at her and added, "No terrible Tribbles."

"How can you call them terrible?" exclaimed Felicity. "It is thanks to Amy and Effy that we are married."

"But you must admit they can be quite ferocious, my sweet. We'll drink a toast to them before we go to bed."

Felicity looked at the very large four-poster bed with the covers turned back. "Now that we are here, Charles," she mumbled against his chest, "things do seem a bit strange and frightening. There are delicate matters the Tribbles' school for manners did not . . . prepare me for."

"I am as nervous as you," he said. "Come, we shall make our discoveries of love together. There are some things, darling Felicity, that you cannot expect two old spinsters to know."

In the house in Holles Street, the two spinster Tribbles toasted each other in champagne, giggled and avoided each other's eyes, as two shocking and unmaidenly Tribble imaginations followed their charge over the last threshold.

"Will it ever be our turn, Amy?" sighed Effy.

"Bound to be," said Amy stoutly. She waved a drunken arm. "Lots of men out there, Effy. Lots and lots. Next year, it'll be our turn, never fear."

Effy turned her face away to hide the sudden glitter of tears in her eyes. That was what Amy always said, Season after Season after Season.

"Mr. Haddon," announced the butler.

Both sisters leaped to their feet. Happiness and dreams were reanimated. While there was a man around, there was still hope.